"What will your friends say?"

"That I'm pretty darned lucky to have found you," Rick stated frankly.

"Not after they discover the unusual circumstances that brought us together."

"It doesn't matter what circumstances brought us together. What matters is that we are together. Why can't you see that it was meant to be? Why can't you let down this invisible barrier you've thrown up between us and see what happens?"

"Because..." Jenny started to answer, but for the life of her could not finish the sentence.

"Jenny, tell me you want me as much as I want you," he said, his voice a tender whisper that fell softly against her cheek.

"I do," she admitted. "I want you very much, but—"

"No buts," he cautioned. "Not now. Not *ever*."

ABOUT THE AUTHOR

For Rosalyn Alsobrook, *Questing Heart* is a very special book. She tells us that "It is my hope that this book will inspire other adoptees to begin their own personal quests. I managed to locate my birth mother. An adoptee cannot imagine the peace of mind or the level of joy he or she will feel once that void from the past has finally been filled."

Rosalyn lives in Texas with her husband and her family.

Books by Rosalyn Alsobrook
HARLEQUIN AMERICAN ROMANCE

63–A TINY FLAW
103–ALL OR NOTHING

Don't miss any of our special offers. Write to us at the following address for information on our newest releases.

Harlequin Reader Service
P.O. Box 1397, Buffalo, NY 14240
Canadian address: P.O. Box 603,
Fort Erie, Ont. L2A 5X3

ROSALYN ALSOBROOK

QUESTING HEART

Harlequin Books

TORONTO • NEW YORK • LONDON
AMSTERDAM • PARIS • SYDNEY • HAMBURG
STOCKHOLM • ATHENS • TOKYO • MILAN

This book is dedicated to my "natural" mom,
Carole Ruth, for having had the love to let me go;
and to my "real" mom, Laura Christine, for having
had the love to take me in; and to Tony, Sheila, and
Shelly for accepting their new "big" sister just like
she was. Also, thanks to everyone who helped me
through my own search (whether they knew they
were helping or not), especially to my own family,
Bobby, Andy, and Tony; and a very *special* thank-
you goes to Reg for allowing me to become a part of
something phenomenal.

Published October 1991

ISBN 0-373-16412-2

QUESTING HEART

Chapter One

Jenny's hands trembled when she reached for the receiver. Her unblinking brown eyes remained focused on the small pad of paper where she had written the telephone number. Slowly she pressed the numbered buttons.

Area code: 9—0—3...

After seven long months she finally had all the information she thought she needed to put her in personal contact with the woman she had been trying so terribly hard to find—the only woman who could answer the many questions that had plagued her off and on throughout the twenty-nine years of her life.

If everything went according to plan during the next few minutes, she would at last discover who she really was and even how she came to be. The possibilities of what she might discover about herself were so endless her blood raced frantic trails through her body, bringing every nerve ending alive.

...5—5—5...

Frightened, yet thrilled at the same time, Jenny glanced at Carole's wide-eyed expression and offered a weak smile. Carole bit deep into the tender flesh of her lower lip and waited for her friend to punch in the last four digits of the telephone number scrawled in large numbers on the pad between them. She knew Carole was almost as nervous about the outcome of this call as she was—*almost*.

. . . 6—6—0. . .

When Jenny rested her fingertip over the final button, she pressed her eyes tightly shut and drew in one last steadying breath. All she had to do was push the tiny button warming beneath the pad of her finger and that would be that. A telephone would ring on the other side of Texas and—and *what?*

All the courage she had fought so hard to build drained out of her like water through a sieve, leaving her feeling weak and empty—and afraid. She couldn't go through with it. Tears blinded her when she slammed the telephone back into its cradle. The possibility of rejection was too real, too terrifying. She was no longer positive she could handle the resulting pain. The stakes were simply too high.

"What are you doing?" Carole wailed.

"I can't go through with it," Jenny said, her lower lip quivering as a result of the hopelessness she felt. She pressed her trembling hands together in an effort to stop their violent shaking, but it did not help. "I just can't do it."

"What do you mean you *can't* do it? Jenny, this is the very moment you've been waiting for." Carole threw up her hands, exasperated. "I thought this was what you wanted, what you worked so hard to accomplish."

"I know. And it is. But I just can't go through with it." She pushed her shoulder-length brown hair away from her face so it would not become caught in the tiny trails of moisture that flowed down her cheeks. Every muscle in her body was still clenched, causing her severe pain. "Carole, what if she hangs up on me? What if she becomes angry with me for suddenly intruding in her life after all these years? It's been almost thirty years since she decided to give me up for adoption. She may not want that part of her past coming back to haunt her now."

Carole sank into the high-backed wooden chair for several seconds, indicating total defeat, then again sat bolt upright. She ran her hand over her face and opened her mouth to speak, but the words did not immediately come.

Leaning forward toward Jenny, who sat directly across from her steeped in utter misery, Carole propped her elbows on the curved edge of the small kitchen table and wagged not one but two fingers at her to indicate that whatever she eventually said would be important.

Finally the words came, and when they did they burst forth in a rush. "Listen to me, Jennifer Lynn Ryan. I didn't go through all that emotional turmoil and constant frustration just to sit here and watch you back out at the last minute. I've been with you on this from the very start. I know everything you had to go through to finally get hold of that one stupid telephone number. I even helped you finagle some of the information you needed by making a few of your telephone calls myself. Geez, girl, you can't quit now! I won't let you!"

"But what if she refuses to talk to me? What if she hears only part of what I have to say and hangs up on me before I can finish saying it?'' With a quick wave of her hand, she indicated the speech she and Carole had so painstakingly perfected.

''What if she *doesn't?*'' Carole asked, shaking her head with such vigor her short blond curls bounced. ''What if she's one of those poor heartbroken women who has been hoping her child would try to find her one day? What if she was one of those who had to give up her baby because of circumstances beyond her control and would give just about anything to know that you are alive and well?''

Oh, please, let that be the case, Jenny pleaded silently. ''But what if she has children of her own, children she didn't have to give up for adoption, children who don't even know I exist?''

''Jen-ni-fer,'' Carole warned, drawing the name out into three slowly pronounced syllables the way she always did whenever she had finally reached that point of total exasperation. ''We've been all through this. If she does have any children, they are surely grown by now. Besides, we both know you wouldn't purposely do anything to cause this woman trouble. If she doesn't want her family to know about you, they don't have to know. Simple as that. Now, will you quit looking for excuses to back out?''

''Okay, okay, I'll call. I *will* call.'' Wetting her lips with a quick dart of her tongue, Jenny reached again for the telephone. Again her hands trembled when she turned the receiver over and placed her fingertips against the first button. Glancing at Carole and seeing the determination radiating from her friend's slate-blue eyes, she felt a devilish urge to torment her. Widening her own eyes in a false display of innocence, she notched her forehead into a slight frown and asked, "Now who was I calling?"

"Jen-ni-fer Lynn Ry-an—" Carole growled. Her hands pressed so hard against the table they turned deathly white at the knuckles.

"Okay, okay. I'm calling. I'm calling," she assured her friend, then glanced again at the telephone number. Although she was able to keep her hands from shaking quite as violently as they had the first time, her foot had taken up a fast, steady rhythm beneath the table. She tapped the heel of her running shoe so rapidly against the vinyl floor and with such an annoying bounce that Carole finally reached beneath the table to forcibly steady the leg.

"Will you calm down?" she whispered softly even though she knew Jenny had yet to complete the call.

"Yeah, right," Jenny muttered with a raised brow while she slowly began pressing the buttons in proper sequence. When she rested her fingertip against that final button, she had to press her eyes closed to help bolster her faltering courage. Only this time she actually pressed the button. Her eyes flew open when she realized she had really done it. She had completed the call.

She was so terrified over what might happen next, the breath she had just sucked in became lodged deep at the base of her throat. She tried to swallow, but the effort did not clear the constriction. Worried she might not be able to speak when the time came, her heart throbbed with painful force, which caused her pulse to hammer loudly in her ears. She barely heard the high tones of the musical code that meant the call was going through.

Again she wet her lips with a quick flick of her tongue and waited for the first ring. Every nerve inside her body pulled taut while she prepared for the absolute worst.

Busy signal!

All the courage and hope drained out of her. The telephone clattered across the table. Her whole body felt limp. She had shot a full week's supply of adrenaline and for nothing.

"What happened?" Carole asked, catching the receiver just before it dropped over the edge, confused by such an unexpected reaction. She leaned across the small table and touched Jenny's cheek with the curve of her hand. "You're not going to faint, are you?"

Suddenly Jenny felt like laughing hysterically, but her body did not have the strength. All she could do was stare numbly into Carole's concerned face. "It was busy."

"Blast!" Carole muttered, letting her head fall back against the top rung of her chair in temporary defeat. "How much more of this can I possibly take?"

"How much more can *you* take?" Jenny asked in disbelief. "What about *me?* What do you think I'm going through? I don't think I can handle anything else going wrong. I'm just about to reach the breaking point."

Carole nodded in understanding. "God sure has His way of testing you to your very limits, that's for sure." She glanced at the clock. "Okay, it's five after eight. We'll give her five minutes, then call back." She smiled in an effort to relieve some of Jenny's tension. "I hope you didn't get your gift for gab from her. If that's the case, it might take us all night to get through.''

Jenny knew that playful jab was meant to ignite a few minutes of lively banter—to help take her mind off the stressful situation—but this time it didn't work. She trained her eyes on the pear-shaped clock near the kitchen sink and watched while the second hand crawled from one second to the next, until finally the five minutes had passed.

Fully prepared for yet a second busy signal, Jenny keyed in the telephone number with less apprehension than before and waited to hear the harsh buzz that meant the call was not yet ready to go through. But this time the buzz did not sound. Her heart bounded to her throat when instead she heard the first ring.

Instantly she grabbed for the handwritten speech she and Carole had worked so hard to compose. Her brown eyes widened and her breath caught deep in her chest while she waited for what seemed an eternity for the second ring. When it came, her right hand closed reflexively into a fist, crumpling the paper with a deafening crunch.

"Is it ringing?" Carole asked, though unnecessarily. It was apparent from Jenny's frightened reaction that it was.

Glancing over at her wide-eyed friend, Jenny nodded and held up two fingers to let her know how many times.

Aware that at any moment someone could answer that phone, it seemed to Jenny that the small kitchen was suddenly devoid of air—yet somehow she managed to keep breathing. While holding the receiver in place against her ear with her shoulder she quickly straightened out the rumpled paper with both hands, smoothing as many of the wrinkles as possible so she could read the words they had so painstakingly written. *Hello, my name is . . .*

The telephone rang again. Jenny wondered if Elizabeth Ellen Anderson would be the one to answer or if someone else would pick up the telephone. Jenny knew it was possible she would have to speak first with the woman's husband or some other member of the family.

Again she glanced down at her speech. *I was born in a special home for unwed mothers in Denton, Texas. My birthday is December 21. The name I was given at birth was . . .*

After having created so many different stories just to obtain some of the important information she needed, it felt good to know she could finally tell the truth. She was searching for her birth mother, a fact that had closed many a friendly mouth.

Even so, if a woman named Elizabeth Ellen Anderson answered that telephone, Jenny would have finally accomplished what she had set out to do. Her quest would be over and she would have at least heard her birth mother's voice.

By the time the telephone rang a fourth time, Jenny's nerves had stretched so tight her whole body ached. Why didn't anyone answer? Someone had to be home. There had been a busy signal!

Swallowing to keep her throat as clear of painful obstructions as possible, considering the circumstances, she glanced down at the papers scattered across the table until she located her birth certificate. Her *original* birth certificate. Without noticing her actions, she lifted her hand and gently touched her birth mother's signature.

At last Jenny heard a click that meant the telephone had been answered. In the following seconds her heart felt as if it might explode.

"Hello?"

It was a male voice. He sounded friendly but tired. Being that late at night, it was understandable he would sound tired. Maybe she should have waited until morning. But that would have been asking the impossible. As Carole had so aptly stated, it was now or never.

"Hello?" the voice repeated, now sounding annoyed that the caller had failed to respond to his initial greeting. "Is anyone there?"

Not knowing who had answered or if he knew anything about her, she reminded herself to be careful and keep her wits about her.

She was not out to hurt anyone. She only wanted to hear her birth mother's voice and possibly be reassured that she had been given up at birth out of necessity. At least Jenny hoped that would be the case. It would break her heart to discover she had been given away at birth simply because she had not been wanted.

She had hurt badly enough last summer when her husband of ten years had suddenly decided he didn't want to be married to her anymore. It would be devastating to learn her own mother had not wanted her either.

"Look, whoever you are, I've got enough problems to deal with right now. If you don't say something immediately, I'm going to hang up," the deep voice warned, his tone threatening.

"Hello, is Elizabeth Anderson in?" she finally asked, amazed at the calm in her voice. She did not as much as breathe while she waited for the response.

"No, she's not," the man answered, still sounding annoyed. "May I take a message?"

Jenny could not remember ever feeling quite so disappointed; yet at the same time, she was extremely excited. She obviously had the correct telephone number—*at last!*

"When will she be in?" she asked. She wondered if she was talking with Elizabeth's husband or possibly her son. Or perhaps they were sufficiently well off to have a butler. She grinned at that last thought, because if the woman had been wealthy she could have afforded to keep her baby.

The unexpected grin threw Carole, causing her eyebrows to drop low with concern. She leaned forward to study Jenny's reactions more carefully.

"Who's calling?" the male voice wanted to know.

Jenny did not know what to answer. She had used so many different identities in the past—whatever had seemed as though it might work at the time—she was now unsure what to say. But this time something inside her warned her to stay as close to the truth as possible. "An old friend of hers."

"You don't sound like an old friend to me," he commented, his tone doubtful.

"Trust me, I am," she responded quickly. "We know each other from way back. When will she be in?"

"I'm her son, Rick. Perhaps I can help you with whatever you need. Or perhaps I can take a message and pass it along to her the next time I see her."

Jenny felt her temper slowly rise. Why couldn't he answer her questions and be done with it? The person she wanted to talk with was Elizabeth. "I'm afraid it's a personal matter. Will she be back later tonight?"

"No," came the simple response. He offered no elaboration, no further conversation.

Jenny was so annoyed by his unwillingness to co-operate, she curled her free hand around the receiver cord until her knuckles turned white. She fought hard to keep the anger out of her voice. She had gone through too much to make a mistake now. "Then when do you expect her? Tomorrow?"

"No," he answered, again with no explanation.

"Then when?" Despite her efforts to remain calm, her voice had started to rise. When she glanced across the table and noticed Carole's bewildered expression, she knew her friend wondered about this sudden display of anger.

"I can't say when," he stated simply.

"You mean you won't say," she muttered, giving up all effort to sound friendly. He was purposely being evasive—and for no apparent reason.

"No, I *can't* say." His voice remained cold and firm. "The doctors don't know when she'll be able to come home again."

Jenny felt a pain so severe and so unexpected she bent forward, pressing her shoulders against the rounded edge of the table to brace herself against further pain. She nearly lost her grip on the receiver. "Why? What happened?"

Her voice had come out a barely audible whisper.

"Until you give me your name and tell me exactly why you are calling, I don't feel at liberty to say."

Jenny had little choice but to give him at least part of the information he sought. She had to know what was wrong with her mother. "Okay. I'll tell you who I am. My name is Jenny. Jennifer Ryan. I live in a small town near Amarillo."

"And?"

"And what? I told you my name and even where I'm from. Now please tell me what has happened to Elizabeth."

"You still haven't said why you're calling," he pointed out.

"I told you. It's personal."

"Until I know something about you, I'm not divulging any further information about my mother. For all I know you are just some saleswoman trying to obtain the sort of personal information you need to trick my mother into buying something she doesn't want or need."

They had reached a stalemate. Jenny didn't dare tell him the real nature of her call for fear she would cause unnecessary problems for her birth mother, and this man was too stubborn to give her even part of the information she wanted until she did. Quickly her brain tried to create a convincing lie, but nothing formulated. All she could contemplate at that moment was what an innate pleasure it would be to strangle this man with his own telephone cord.

"I'm sorry, Miss Ryan, or whoever you are. But I don't have time for any more games. I have to be at the hospital by nine, if I want to see my mother tonight.

They are very strict about their visiting hours. Goodbye.'' Those sharp words were followed by a deafening click.

Jenny sat staring numbly at Carole, the receiver still gripped tightly in her hand. After several seconds she finally lowered it toward the table, then placed it gently onto the base.

"What happened?" Carole demanded, casting her gaze to the telephone as if she might find the answers lying before her in plain sight. "Who was that?"

"My half brother," she stated, her voice low and monotoned. "He claims my mother is in the hospital, but refused to tell me what was wrong with her."

"Why would he do that?" Carole wanted to know. She came immediately out of her chair and placed a supportive arm around Jenny's slumped shoulders. "Oh, you poor dear."

Jenny's mind was a whirling mass of anger, confusion and fear. "What if she's dying, Carole? What if she's dying and I'm never given the chance to talk with her?"

Carole seemed not to know what to say. "What are you going to do?"

"I have to go there. I have to try to see her."

Carole nodded that she understood. "I'll call Howard for you and explain to him that you won't be there tomorrow night."

"Graduation! I forgot all about that. I'm supposed to hand out the diplomas."

"I know. But they can always find someone else to do that. After all, how much talent does it take to pick up those rolled pieces of paper one at a time and hand them to the passing students? Even I could manage that."

"Would you? Would you take my place? I'd feel much better about leaving if I knew there was already someone to take my place. And I really would like to take the very next flight headed to East Texas."

"As long as Howard doesn't mind, I don't," Carole assured her. "And you know what we've always said about that man. He's a principal without any principles, so I don't think he'll mind letting me do the honors instead of you. I'll call him right now. Then I'll call the airport for you. You go get your things packed."

Jenny hurried to her bedroom, so frantic with concern she could not think where to begin. Jerking down two suitcases, she started flinging her clothes haphazardly into them. After several minutes Carole came into the room with the next bit of bad news.

"I squared everything with Howard. He was actually very understanding about it, even said he'd handle any last-minute requests for transcripts and college entrance forms. He wished you luck and a safe flight. But when I called the airport I was told the next flight that can possibly land you anywhere near Tyler won't leave Amarillo until eleven tomorrow morning, and it has a two-hour layover at Dallas/Fort Worth. That won't put you into Tyler until sometime after two o'clock."

Jenny felt as if the entire world was working against her. "I may as well drive."

"You'd get there just as quick, if not a little quicker," Carole agreed. "I already checked it on the map. If you left right away and stopped only when you had to, I think you could probably be there as early as noon tomorrow."

"Then that's what I'll do. At least I'll still have the use of my car after I get there," she said, trying her best to look at the brighter side, which was something she normally encouraged her students to do. "Would you do me one more favor?"

"Go fill your car with gas," Carole commented. "I have never known you to have a full tank when you needed it. Where are the keys?"

"On top of the refrigerator," Jenny told her, even though Carole knew that was where she always kept them. "Meanwhile I'll change into something more appropriate and finish packing."

By the time Carole returned from the only all-night gas station in the area, which was halfway to Amarillo, Jenny had finished dressing and packing and was busily pacing the floor, trying to think of anything she might need that she had forgotten in her haste.

"Ready?" Carole asked, eyeing first the yellow-and-white dress Jenny wore and then the closed suitcases with surprise.

"I guess. I know I'm forgetting something important, but for the life of me I can't figure out what it might be."

Carole tapped her finger against her pursed lips while she called out some of the more obvious things Jenny would need. When Jenny nodded affirmative to each one, Carole shrugged. "Then I think you have everything. Oh, what about your birth certificate? You might need that to prove to those people you really are who you say you are."

That was a good idea. Jenny hurried to the kitchen table to retrieve the document and also picked up the paper on which she'd written her birth mother's telephone number. Ever so gently she folded the two papers in half and tucked them into the side of her purse. "What else?"

"Look, it's not like you are leaving the planet. If you forget something important, I can always express it to you. I've still got a key to this place, you know," Carole said, seeming eager for Jenny to be on her way. "Just you remember to call me and let me know where I can reach you and how everything turns out. Because if you don't call me and tell me absolutely everything, you'll regret it for the rest of your short life."

Jenny chuckled at Carole's none too subtle warning, knowing it was meant to make her laugh, thereby calming her frazzled nerves. "Water my plants while I'm gone," she said, tucking her purse under her arm and looking around the kitchen one last time, still certain she was forgetting something important.

"Will do. Now go."

"Bring in my newspapers and collect my mail."

"Will do. Now *go.*"

"Feed Walter, Jr. for me."

"I'll see to it that your mindless mutt has more food than he ever dreamed possible," Carole promised, then crossed her arms over the soft material of her pale pink sweatshirt and tapped her running shoes impatiently. "Now, go!"

Jenny was not surprised to find the car still running and the door open when she stepped outside with her two suitcases. Once a decision had been made, Carole was not one to turn her back on it. Jenny hurried down the steps. "I'll call."

"You bet you will. Remember? Your life depends on it," Carole commented, leaning far inside the driver's door to push the trunk release, then hurriedly helping Jenny situate the two bulky suitcases inside the small trunk.

As soon as Carole had them where they would not jostle back and forth during travel, she slammed the trunk lid down, then turned to embrace her friend. Tears filled her eyes but she did nothing to hide them.

"Remember not to let your emotions become too involved," she warned, blinking rapidly as she bent forward for her farewell hug. "You've been hurt enough here lately." She then straightened and sniffed indelicately. "Good luck, Jen."

Jenny was still blinking back tears when she pulled out of the driveway, and several times during the next fourteen hours she caught herself sobbing aloud for no apparent reason.

Because most of the roads across northern Texas were under construction at that time—or so it seemed to Jenny—it was after one o'clock before she finally arrived in Tyler, Texas.

Since it was such a cool day for early June, she had traveled the last few hours of her trip with her window down and her sunroof up. The fresh air and the sweet scent of the pine trees and rosebushes that were so prominent in East Texas helped her keep her straying thoughts where she wanted them: away from all the many fears and the recurring frustration that tormented her. But now that she was finally there, finally in the same town with her birth mother, the throbbing pain deep in the hollow of her chest had returned.

What if she was too late?

She refused to consider that possibility for long. God had not permitted her to accomplish all she had accomplished over the past few months, then travel all that way unharmed, just to allow something so tragic to happen. No, it would all work out. It had to. She would finally be allowed to meet the woman who had given birth to her and learn all there was to know about herself.

Or would she?

If only she could be sure.

Having already thought through her initial plan of action, Jenny stopped at the first pay telephone she found that still had a telephone directory attached. With trembling hands, she fumbled through the Yellow Pages until she found the listing for hospitals. There were three major hospitals and a large cancer-treatment center in Tyler.

Setting the book to one side while still open to the correct page, she called the first number listed. No Elizabeth Anderson there. She called the second one and was relieved to be told, yes, Elizabeth Anderson was a patient there; yet at the same time she was horrified because the woman's next words had been, "She's in ICU."

"Could you tell me how serious her illness is?"

"No, I'm afraid I can't. We are not allowed to give out that sort of information over the telephone. I'm sorry."

"That's all right. I understand." And she did. She had expected it. It had been the same back when her adoptive parents had had their automobile accident. She'd had to go directly to the hospital before she could find out exactly how serious the accident had been. Therefore she decided her next move should be to find a Tyler map and pinpoint the location of that hospital. Quickly she jotted down the address from the directory, then returned to her car to find a place that sold local maps.

Having gotten caught in a tangle of one-way streets that all seemed to be going the wrong way close to the main part of town, it was shortly after three before she finally located the hospital. It was fifteen after the hour by the time she found an empty space to park. She lost another five minutes by taking the time to touch up her makeup before making the half-block walk to the main entrance. If something did happen that finally allowed her to meet her birth mother, she wanted to look her very best.

After stepping inside and asking a woman dressed in a pink-and-white uniform of a volunteer where she might obtain information concerning patients in ICU, Jenny was directed down a maze of stark gray corridors where she eventually found the appropriate nurses' station for those patients confined to ICU.

"May I help you?" a square-shouldered nurse in a starched white uniform asked when she glanced up from her paperwork and noticed Jenny standing at her window.

"Yes, please. My name is Jenny Ryan. I would like to know how Elizabeth Anderson is."

The nurse pushed her thick-framed glasses higher onto her nose with the back of her wrist, then peered at Jenny through the lower portion of the heavy lenses. "And are you a member of the immediate family?"

Jenny felt a wave of foreboding chills cascade down her neck and across her shoulders—a direct result of the cold, disapproving manner in which the woman stared at her. Jenny had a strong suspicion this woman already knew the answer to that question. "No, I'm not exactly part of the immediate family. But I am a very close friend."

"I see. Well, I'm sorry, but I cannot give out that sort of information except to immediate family," she said, already turning a shoulder to her as she lifted her pen to resume her paperwork. "You'll have to speak with one of them."

"Are any of them here?" She glanced around to see if she could locate a nearby waiting area for the people with family in ICU.

"No," she answered simply, not bothering to look at Jenny again.

Jenny tapped her high heel against the gray tile floor impatiently. She'd about had it with rude people. "Well, then, may I at least speak with her doctor?"

"Suit yourself. This is Wednesday," she said, glancing at the inside of her wrist, where she kept the face of her watch. "He should be in here around six."

Jenny did not think she could bear having to wait that long to find out anything. She wondered if it might help to try to contact the doctor's office first by telephone. "Who is her doctor?"

There was a short pause, as if the nurse was not at all certain she wanted to give out even that much information. Finally she answered. "Dr. Weathers. Dr. Lowell Weathers." She shrugged her ample shoulders and then peered again at Jenny through the lower portion of her eyeglasses. This time there was a little less contempt in her voice. "But he'll just tell you the same thing I've already told you. That sort of information can only be given to members of the immediate family. It's hospital policy."

"Well, can I at least visit with her for a minute?" No sooner had Jenny spoken the words than she questioned whether that would be such a good idea. She did not know enough about Elizabeth Anderson's condition to know if this would be an appropriate time to announce herself or not.

The nurse immediately shook her head. "No. It is also hospital policy that only immediate family can visit the patients in ICU. And even family members are restricted to two visitors at a time and only ten minutes per visiting period. Your best bet is to get hold of her only son, Rick, and ask him for the information you want. He keeps up with every little change in her condition."

Frustrated from knowing, in all actuality, she *was* immediate family, but not about to impart that bit of information without first having her birth mother's consent to do so, Jenny heaved a weary sigh. "What if I explained to you that I've come a long, long way to see her—that I've just traveled all the way across Texas, from the panhandle. Would that sway you in any way?"

"No, ma'am."

She thought not.

Finally the nurse's tone softened and Jenny saw the first indication the woman possessed any real compassion at all.

"Look, rules are rules. I don't make them. I just enforce them. That's part of my job. If you want to know what Liz's condition is, you'll have to talk with Rick."

Liz? Evidently this nurse knew her birth mother personally, which made Jenny's situation all the more impossible. This woman was not about to do anything that might hurt her friend. That left only one option open. Somehow, she had to convince the man with that angry voice whom she had spoken to on the telephone earlier to tell her what she wanted to know.

Suddenly Jenny felt as if she had swallowed a stomachful of cold lead.

Chapter Two

By the time Jenny had left the ICU area, "Nurse Stoneface" had finally admitted there was a possibility, however slight, that she might be allowed in to see Elizabeth—if she returned with both Rick's and the doctor's written approval. But she had to have both to be allowed into her room.

With renewed hope, Jenny hurried along the brightly lit corridors, retracing her footsteps over the shiny gray tile until she again found the door that led to the main parking lot. She wanted to locate her half brother while she still had the courage to ask him for his help. As long as there remained even the slightest possibility that she might be allowed in to see her mother, she had to try.

As quickly as her high heels would permit on the uneven pavement, she wove her way through the crowded parking lot, while the nurse's parting words echoed in the back of her mind, fortifying her determination.

"I guess if you did manage to get both of them to approve, in writing so no one gets in any trouble, you might be allowed a few minutes with her," the nurse had finally confessed, however reluctantly. "Even though technically you are not a part of the woman's immediate family and the rules say you really should not be allowed in unless you are a close relative, it still might be possible for you to see her."

Well, *technically* Jenny knew she *was* a part of Elizabeth Anderson's immediate family; yet *legally* she wasn't. But having been unable to impart that bit of information to the iron-willed nurse, Jenny had no other option open to her. She would have to locate Rick Anderson and beg for his cooperation.

After stopping at the telephones in the hall near the main lobby long enough to look up Rick's home address and his telephone number in one of the local directories, the first thing she did after returning to her car was consult her map and find the location of 1607 Pineway.

Jenny was surprised to discover her half brother's house was only a few blocks away. Considering how many of the other events during the past twenty-four hours had gone, she'd halfway expected to find that it was somewhere in the next county.

Glancing at the digital clock above her radio, she noticed that the time was not yet five o'clock. If her half brother worked, which she supposed he did, it was likely he was not yet home.

Whether she was troubled over the thought of having to confront the man behind the angry voice she'd encountered the previous night, or whether out of common courtesy to someone who would no doubt come home tired and in need of a few moments of relaxation, Jenny decided not to go straight to Pineway.

Curious to see where her birth mother lived, she chose to locate her house first. She also knew there was a chance Rick might be there instead of at his own home, because that was where she had caught him the evening before, at their mother's house.

Because Elizabeth Anderson's home was also not very far from the hospital, Jenny had located the place within minutes. She was immediately impressed with both the size of the house and the elegance of the surrounding neighborhood. It had never occurred to her that the woman might be wealthy.

Jenny was not exactly sure why, but she had always thought of her birth mother as poor and struggling. Perhaps because being financially unable to provide for a child would have been a logical reason for giving her up for adoption in the first place.

It confused and disappointed Jenny to see such obvious wealth. The house was enormous—a stately three-story Victorian nestled into an entire half block of tall, lumbering oak trees and surrounded by perfectly sculptured landscape. She decided the woman must have married into money. She refused to believe her biological mother had been born wealthy. Her pride simply would not allow it.

A full hour passed before Jenny grew at all tired of staring at the huge house and trying to imagine the people who lived there. After having memorized everything about the outside of the house, she restarted her engine and headed back toward the area where her half brother lived.

She was ready to approach Rick Anderson with her plea. Although she realized she still chanced disturbing his dinner hour by stopping by so shortly after six, she had reached the emotional apex where she had to get the initial confrontation over with or lose her mind. Again, it was now or never, and she just could not face the possibility of never. Not after all she had gone through.

After consulting her street map one last time to make certain she had located the correct neighborhood, she headed straight for Pineway, as determined as ever to be done with it.

When she pulled her silver-gray Grand Am to a slow stop in front of the curb marked 1607 with bold black numbers, she was again surprised by the grandeur. Even the son had money.

Although Jenny had grown up in a nice home and in a nice neighborhood, with a large backyard and plenty of trees and flower gardens, it had been nothing like this. Rick Anderson's house was like his mother's in that it was also three stories tall, but Rick's house was far more modern in design. Yet it, too, had been built in a secluded neighborhood and stood on an entire half block of land.

Staring at the house she tried to guess the size of Rick's family, wondering if she had any unexpected nieces and nephews. Rick had to have at least half a dozen children to fill such a large, sprawling house. She then stared at the tall privacy fence near the back, wondering if it surrounded a huge backyard filled with an elaborate array of swings, seesaws and jungle gyms, or perhaps his children were older and it hid an impressive swimming pool with a large deck area where the family relaxed together during the evenings and on weekends. But there was no way for her to be sure what was back there because the fence stood a full ten feet in height.

Deciding she needed to make the very best first impression possible, especially after seeing how well these people lived, Jenny opened her purse and pulled out first her brush, then her compact. While she quickly reworked her hair and touched up the shiny areas of her makeup for the second time that day she felt her first real pangs of excitement, for she was about to meet her half brother. He might be a grump when talking on the telephone—and with their mother so ill in the hospital, he had every right to be—but grump or no grump, he was still her brother.

By the time Jenny had placed everything back into her purse and had resnapped it, her hands were trembling again and her pulse raced with so many different emotions it would take a week to sort them out.

When she opened the car door and stepped out onto the street, she discovered that her knees felt wobbly. She knew that whatever transpired during those next few minutes could mean the difference between finally being allowed to meet the woman who had given birth to her or being forced to leave town without ever having known her. The result of this visit with her half brother was vital. She simply had to win his approval and win it right away.

By the time Jenny finally stood before the huge double doors, she felt as if she was on the verge of having a full-fledged heart attack. It seemed unlikely she could survive such a ferocious pounding for very long.

Courageously she took a deep breath to cushion her thudding heart and held it in place while she knocked, all the while wondering if her chest would explode from the strain before anyone bothered to answer.

Expecting to be greeted at the door by a man who resembled her in many ways—only younger—Jenny pushed the leather strap of her handbag high onto her shoulder and continued facing the door, her body rigidly erect. When there was no immediate response, she noticed a lighted doorbell off to one side and leaned over to press it. Her stomach was a jumbled mass of fear and expectation by the time she heard the steady rhythm of footsteps from within.

When the right half of the front door finally swung open, she was surprised and a little disappointed to be met by a tall blond man dressed in faded blue jeans and a pale blue cotton shirt that he had not bothered to button or tuck in. She tried not to notice the springy body hair that covered his bared chest and lean stomach just before she turned her attention to the medium length of his honey-colored hair and the long light brown eyelashes surrounding his pale blue eyes.

Jenny was disappointed. This man was the exact opposite of her; even his facial details were different. His nose was long and straight, his jaw wide and solid and his dark blond eyebrows thick.

Although he was undeniably handsome, she knew she could never claim him to be her half brother. His physical appearance was just too different. Her hair and eyes were dark brown, her nose short and turned up at the end. Her jawline was a lot narrower and her eyebrows much darker, thinner and shaped entirely differently.

Even the curves of their cheeks and the width of their foreheads were different. Besides, this man had to be in his early thirties and that made him older than her. She decided he was probably an older friend of Rick's, which meant she would do well to win him over to her side immediately. She smiled her most winning smile, the one that usually charmed even the most obstinate of students.

But the smile had no effect on him. Instead of returning her smile, he frowned, then glanced out into the yard, as if expecting to find someone else.

Jenny did not hesitate, aware if she did she would never get the words out. She spoke while offering her hand.

"Hello, my name is Jennifer Ryan. May I speak with Rick Anderson, please?" She kept her cordial smile while already glancing past the man to see if anyone else stood nearby, eager to get her first glimpse of her half brother.

"Ryan?" he asked, puzzled by the name, then suddenly his face registered recognition. "Oh, you're the one who called Mother's house last night while I was there watering her plants and checking her mail. You're that young lady who dared to telephone so late, then refused to leave a message or even say why she'd called."

Jenny's eyes widened. "You? You're Rick Anderson?" She again appraised the differences between them. He couldn't be. He was too old. His eyes were too blue. And his temperament was too hostile.

"Yes, I'm Rick Anderson," he said, verifying her worst fears. "I'm Elizabeth Anderson's son."

Jenny was so disappointed over the discovery they looked nothing alike, she was at a temporary loss for words. All she could do was stand there, dumbstruck, searching his face for some noticeable resemblance, some clue that would assure her she had indeed found her half brother.

"I—I'd like a word with you. May I come inside?"

He studied her a moment, then apparently decided she offered no real threat and stepped back to let her enter. As an afterthought, he reached for the lower part of his shirt and quickly fastened the bottom three buttons, leaving a vast amount of lean muscles and body hair still exposed to her view.

"Whatever it is, make it quick. My daughter is late returning from softball practice, and if she doesn't come marching through that door within the next five minutes I'm going to have to go out looking for her."

His entire body tensed while he spoke, letting Jenny know he was more angry than worried over his daughter's absence.

So, he does have a family. Jenny made a quick mental note, aware she had at least one niece, possibly more. Suddenly she worried what that niece would think of her if the girl ever learned the truth. What were *all* of these people going to think of her?

"Well, if this is not a good time to—" Jenny said, hesitating. She would prefer to have their talk when he was in a better mood, perhaps after the daughter had returned and apologized for being so late.

She fought the urge to shove her hands into the hidden pockets of the wide-skirted yellow-and-white dress she had chosen to wear.

"Actually this is as good a time as any," he admitted with a disgruntled shake of his head. He gently closed the door behind her, then indicated another door off to her right with a quick sideward nod of his head. "Just what is it you want to talk to me about?"

Remembering that the subject had already proven to be a sore one with him, she waited until they were inside the large, elegantly decorated sitting room and she had lowered herself into the nearest chair. Glad to be off her shaky legs, she turned her gaze to his, expecting him to sit, too. "I've come here hoping to find out more about your mother. I've been worried sick about her ever since you told me she was ill."

Rick tilted his head to one side, carefully studying her while he stepped back and rested casually against the rounded arm of a small sofa. "And just who are you?"

"I told you. I'm Jenny Ryan. I'm an old friend of your mother's and I'm very, very concerned about her."

He continued to study her for another long moment, then straightened his head and asked, "Why is it I've never heard of you before now?"

"I'm not sure," she admitted, finding his bold perusal a little annoying.

His eyebrows lifted while he pursed his lips into a thoughtful frown. Slowly his eyebrows lowered again and he cast a glance at a large porcelain clock that sat on the fireplace mantel. He then glanced at his watch as if unwilling to believe the clock was correct.

Jenny noticed his distraction, aware he was dividing his attention between what she had to say and the fact his daughter had yet to come home. She took advantage of the momentary distraction and studied him for a few seconds.

Although Rick was without a doubt a very handsome man, one she would be proud to claim as her brother, she still found it hard to believe they were in any way related. He was just too different from her. But in all fairness, even full-blood brothers and sisters did not always resemble each other—and she and Rick had only one parent in common.

Still the difference between them had caused her to suffer her first doubts since her arrival in Tyler. Perhaps she had located the wrong Elizabeth Anderson after all. That thought brought a sheen of tears to her eyes. What if her search was not yet nearing its end as she had so hoped? What if she had followed a false trail?

"How long have you known my mother?" he asked, when his thoughts finally returned to what happened around him.

"Since I was a child."

"Then why is it we have never met?" he asked. His forehead wrinkled while he studied her again. "You don't look at all familiar to me." He then glanced at his watch again.

"I'm sorry," she finally said, aware she had timed this all wrong. "I realize this is a bad time for you. I'd like to make this quick. If you would just be so kind as to tell me what I want to know about Elizabeth, I'll gladly be on my way."

He dropped his wrist and looked at her again, wondering why she was in such a rush. It bothered him enough that Rachel was so late, but it bothered him even more that this pretty young stranger pretended to know his mother, when he was certain she didn't.

He had never as much as heard her name before last night, nor had he seen a photograph of her, and his mother was the type who kept photographs of practically everyone she knew.

If he had seen a photograph of her, he would remember. She had the sort of face one could not easily forget—pretty to the point of being beautiful and even somewhat beguiling, yet full of a strange sort of wide-eyed innocence—or at least that was how she wanted to appear—young and innocent.

"No, *Miss Ryan.*" He glanced at her wedding finger to see if he had labeled her correctly and was oddly pleased to find no ring. "I am not about to tell you anything until you finally explain to me why you think you have some right to meddle in my mother's life."

He still suspected her to be some sort of saleswoman trying to get the inside track. And if that was the case, especially when she knew the seriousness of his family's present circumstances, he would gladly toss her out on her ear—pretty or not.

"I'm not trying to meddle in anything," she quickly assured him. "All I really want to do is find out how serious your mother's illness is. That, and I would also like your permission to visit her in the hospital if and when she feels up to it."

"If you are such a good friend and are so concerned about her, then why don't you just tell me how you know her?" Although she had sounded sincerely concerned and seemed relatively harmless, he still did not trust her. After all, even his own ex-wife had seemed harmless enough when he'd first met her. Obviously he was a poor judge of women.

"I can't tell you that," she said, knowing what sort of trouble it might cause.

"Can't or won't?"

"Both," she finally admitted. "Please, just believe me when I tell you, I am not out to harm her in any way."

"I find it hard to believe anything you say," he stated, crossing his arms, as if challenging her. "Why should I believe you? You are a total stranger to me."

That was true enough. She was a total stranger to him and there was no getting around that. "But I am a stranger who cares very much about your mother."

"And how do I know that? For all I know, you could be a pathological liar eager to cause trouble wherever you can."

Jenny sighed. What could she say to convince him? "I'm not out to cause any trouble. I told you that." Again, she and her half brother had reached a stalemate. Again, he stubbornly refused to give her the information she wanted until he knew more about her, and until she had talked with her birth mother and had been granted permission to discuss such a delicate matter, she was unable to provide the information he wanted. "Please, just tell me how serious her condition is. What harm could that cause?"

He tapped his fingers against the soft blue material that covered his well-muscled arms while he thought about that. His deep blue eyes narrowed, as if hoping to see right through her. "I don't like people who intentionally keep secrets from me, and you, my dear Miss Ryan, are doing just that. Why should I bother to tell you what you want to know when you have flatly refused to tell me what I want to know?"

Jenny glared at him, her expression hardening. He certainly topped the list for being the most difficult man she had ever encountered—except perhaps for her ex-husband. In fact, that was who Rick had started to remind her of—*Robert*.

The more Jenny got to know Rick, the more she believed him to be every bit as arrogant and every bit as overbearing as her ex-husband, Robert—if not more so—and just as stubborn. She realized Rick would have to be dealt with carefully, if she ever hoped to make him an ally. "And what if I told you that my relationship with your mother might be something she would not want revealed?"

That took him by surprise. He looked at her, truly puzzled now. He had opened his mouth as if ready to ask yet another question, when suddenly the front door banged open and he turned his attention immediately to the noise.

"Rachel? Come here right now!" he commanded, his voice stern, as he headed for the hallway door. "I want to know why you are so late."

Aware she had been temporarily forgotten, Jenny turned to face the doorway and watched while a pretty, yet disheveled thirteen-year-old girl appeared in the doorway. Jenny knew, by the color of her long blond hair and her angry blue eyes, that this was definitely Rick's daughter. They looked so much alike, it was uncanny.

"I told you, I had softball practice today," she said, none too politely. She tucked a well-worn baseball glove under her arm and then leaned indolently against the doorjamb.

"Baseball practice was over with well over an hour ago," he informed her, glancing at his watch, verifying the time.

"And how do you know that?" She narrowed her eyes accusingly as she thrust her chin forward to show she resented his having that knowledge.

"When you didn't come home right away, I called Shelly's house. She told me that practice was already over and that you should be home any minute. When you weren't I then called Sheila's house to make sure you hadn't stopped by there, and she told me you hadn't."

"So you've been checking up on me again," she complained as she glowered angrily at him. She glanced then at Jenny, but seemed little interested in the fact a stranger was in the house and obviously able to hear everything she and her father had to say. "That figures!"

Rick took a deep breath, curling his hands into hard fists at his sides. "I was worried when you didn't come home. Especially after I had reminded you twice this morning to get back here as quickly as you possibly could so we could make the seven o'clock visiting time. You know how your grandmother loves to see you."

"So I forgot and stopped by the Whataburger for a shake," she said, squaring her jaw as if daring him to do anything about it. "We can still make the nine o'clock visiting hour. It's not like she's going to die within the next hour or so."

The mention of death caused Jenny's stomach to knot with sudden fear. She had been unable to determine if the girl had made such a frightful comment out of sheer spite toward her father, or whether there was a real possibility that Elizabeth was about to die.

"That's not the point," Rick responded, shaking his head with warning. "The point is that I asked you to come straight home after practice and you disobeyed me."

"So shoot me," she said in a raised voice and rolled her blue eyes upward, as if unable to see any reason for him to be so concerned.

"Don't tempt me," Rick bit back.

Jenny felt increasingly uncomfortable while she watched the angry exchange between father and daughter. She wondered what had caused such hostile feelings between the two. There had to be deeply set underlying reasons for them both to be this angry at one another.

Jenny frowned while she studied the two more closely. This was more than a teenager rebelling against authority; there had been true resentment in this girl's voice. Jenny wondered if Rachel also behaved that hatefully toward her mother, or had this temperamental display been strictly for her father's benefit.

Jenny was curious about where Rick's wife might be. Obviously she was not in the house. A loud argument like that would have brought any wife and mother on the run.

Rick glanced back over his shoulder as if suddenly remembering someone else was in the room. Jenny saw the pain in his expression and realized how vulnerable he was when it came to his rebellious daughter. Suddenly he seemed a little more human.

"I guess I'd better go," she said, slipping the strap of her handbag over her shoulder but not yet rising from her chair. "I'll come back later."

"No, stay." He frowned while his gaze darted back and forth between his daughter and Jenny. Clearly he was torn between allowing her to leave before the argument became any worse and wanting her to stay. "You were about to tell me something about your relationship with my mother. I want to hear that."

"Fine," Rachel said, stiffening with a jolt. "I'll be waiting in my room whenever you think you're finally ready to go to the hospital."

"Take a bath first," he warned, watching while she hurriedly stalked off toward the stairs.

"Fine," came the distant response. "I'll take a bath. Anything else?"

His shoulders tensed perceptibly. "Just that I'd like to see a big change in your attitude before we go."

"Okay, fine," she called out, far enough away that Jenny barely heard her.

Rick immediately turned to face Jenny. "I apologize for Rachel's behavior. She's been a little difficult ever since the—" Then as if he realized that his daughter's rude behavior was none of Jenny's business, he seemed to change his mind about what he was going to say. "So, tell me, what is your relationship with my mother?"

Jenny studied his determined expression for several seconds. "You aren't going to tell me anything about her condition until you know, are you?"

"No. I'm not." He crossed his arms to show he was serious.

Aware of her dilemma, Jenny bit into the sensitive inner flesh of her lower lip while she considered what to do. If she continued to deny him the information he wanted, he would continue to deny her the information she wanted. Yet if she told him the truth without having discussed it with her mother first, she might be alienating the woman forever. If only she knew exactly how serious Elizabeth's illness was, then she could decide if she was on the verge of losing her only chance to ever speak with her.

Jenny studied his stern expression a moment longer, already aware of what she had to do, and already knowing the worst between them was yet to come. It broke her heart to know that although she desperately wanted her half brother to be her ally, Fate had already placed them on opposing sides.

"Okay, I'll tell you," she finally said, knowing it was the only way. She just hoped her birth mother would understand why she had had to reveal her secret and would one day find it in her heart to forgive her.

Rick heaved an audible sigh and unfolded his arms while he waited for her to continue.

"You asked what my relationship is to your mother." She hesitated, wondering what his reaction would be. "Well, I'm her daughter."

Rick's facial muscles hardened again and his blue eyes glittered with renewed anger. "Yeah, right. And I'm the tooth fairy." He then pointed toward the door. "Listen, I don't know what your game is, but this is my house and I don't have to stand here and listen to this garbage. Get out of here—now! Before I decide to call the police." His eyes widened over what he'd just said. "Maybe that is what I ought to do. Call the police. Maybe they can figure out what it is you're up to." He then headed for the telephone, his expression grim with determination.

Chapter Three

"No, don't call the police!" she pleaded, coming immediately out of the chair. "This is something your mother might not want anyone to know about, at least not yet."

Rick paused with his hand rigid over the receiver and glowered at her. "You mean this is something *you* don't want the police to know about."

"No, that's not entirely true," she said, watching to see if he still intended to pick up the telephone. "Please, at least give me a chance to explain."

"I don't think I want to hear any of your explanations," he said, his voice chilled with resentment.

"Well, isn't that just like a man," she snapped, again reminded of her ex-husband. "Afraid to hear the truth, are you?"

Evidently she'd struck a nerve because his hand came off the telephone and he pointed an accusing finger at her. "Nothing you have to say is the truth. And nothing you can say or do will ever convince me that it is."

And *that* was probably the truth, too. Jenny had never been able to change Robert's opinion with mere words or simple actions, either. "What if I *show* you something that will prove without a doubt that what I have said is true?"

"And what might that be?" he asked, clearly questioning her ability to produce anything that would convince him of something so outrageous.

"My birth certificate," she said and lowered her handbag onto the table beside the telephone. When she snapped open the clasp and reached inside, she noticed he tensed and had immediately focused his attention on the movements of her hand. "Don't worry. I'm not carrying a pistol or anything dangerous."

Obviously that was not what had bothered him, for he remained extremely rigid despite her reassurances.

"I'm going to pull out my birth certificate so I can show you that I'm telling the truth. I am your mother's daughter."

He waited, not moving so much as a muscle while she carefully slipped the folded piece of paper out of her purse and then handed it to him.

"Here."

He accepted the heavy textured paper with his thumb and fingertips, as if he had expected it to be made of something harmful. Gently he unfolded the page, never taking his gaze off hers. When he finally had it unfolded, he glanced down and read the first section. His eyes widened when he glanced to the next section and caught a glimpse of the signature. When he looked at Jenny again, his confused expression revealed he now had doubts but was still not truly convinced.

Jenny leaned forward and pointed to the document. "As you can see, your mother is also my mother. We may have had different fathers, but we definitely have the same mother." For the first time since entering the house, she smiled. "I'm your half sister."

He shook his head, his face unreadable. "No, you are not. Even if this certificate is real—and I'm not at all sure that it is—you are not my half sister. You and I are in no way related."

"Sure we are," she said and felt the beginning traces of tears at the outer corners of her eyes. She refused to be denied her heritage. "The very same woman gave birth to both of us."

"Even if this is real—" he again indicated the paper he held with a look of distrust "—you are not my half sister." His expression darkened. "Elizabeth Anderson is not my biological mother. I was adopted at the age of four."

Now it was Jenny's turn to stare at him, stunned. No wonder they did not look anything alike. "But I don't understand. Why would she adopt when she could have had children of her own?"

"That's just it. She couldn't." Again he sounded skeptical, almost accusing. "She had a swimming accident when she was still a teenager that left her unable to have any of her own children—*ever!*"

Again Jenny experienced doubts. Had she made a mistake? Could she have the wrong Elizabeth Anderson? "How old was she when this happened?"

"Eighteen," he remembered, running his hand through his blond hair while he tried to recollect the exact date. "It was during the summer, right after she had graduated from high school."

Jenny felt a surge of relief, though it pained her to know how her mother must have suffered. "She had me when she was seventeen."

"How do you know that?" He glanced at the birth certificate to see if it revealed her age.

"I have most of my birth records."

"Let's see them." He looked at her purse, as if waiting for her to produce more evidence.

"I don't have them with me."

Rick cocked his head to one side and raised a skeptical eyebrow. "How convenient."

Jenny did not like his arrogant attitude and fought to keep her anger in check. "I didn't think I'd need them. After all, I brought my birth certificate. I thought that would be proof enough but if you'd like I can have a friend of mine express them to me. I could have them here day after tomorrow."

Rick glanced down at the signature again and felt a cold, prickling feeling along the back of his neck. The similarity between that signature and his mother's caused a sinking ache in the pit of his stomach. He looked at Jenny closely and noticed she even resembled his mother—in many ways. But that could be a coincidence.

Jenny waited several seconds to give him time to absorb some of what he had learned before mentioning again her main reason for being there. "Will you now agree to go with me to the hospital, so I can meet her?"

"No," he answered immediately. That was the only thing he was certain about at that moment. Even if this young woman spoke the truth, his mother was in no shape to have something like this sprung on her.

"But that's not fair," she protested. "How can you be so selfish?"

"I'm not selfish," he stated. His desire to protect his mother had come to the forefront. "I am practical. At the moment, my mother is extremely ill—" His shoulders tensed when she interrupted him.

"*Our* mother," she corrected, determined that he at least admit that much.

"Whether or not she should be called *our* mother has yet to be proven, at least as far as I'm concerned. And even if you are who you claim to be, Mother does not need that sort of emotional strain troubling her— not if she is ever to get out of the hospital."

More out of anger than anything else, Jenny jutted her chin forward and crossed her arms in a clear show of defiance. "I have every right to see my own mother, if I want."

"I'm not sure if you have any rights at all here," he responded quickly, feeling more and more threatened. He was still too overwhelmed by the fact his mother might have secretly had a child out of wedlock so many years ago to make any complicated decisions at the moment. If it was true, if his mother had indeed had a child when she was seventeen, why had she never told him? They had always had such an open relationship. Which was why this all seemed a little too farfetched. "How do I even know that is a real birth certificate?"

"By the fact it has been certified at the bottom by the state registrar," she said, irritated that he had yet to accept the truth. "And by the signature right there under the word Informant.'' She leaned forward to point out the location of their mother's own signature on the certificate.

"I'm clever enough to know this could be forged," he said, despite the knowledge that it was very similar to his mother's present signature. And there was also the matter of the physical resemblance of this woman and his mother, especially remembering how his mother had looked during her younger years. They both had the same eyes, the same general facial structure. They even shared a few of the same mannerisms, like the way they both chewed nervously on the right side of their lower lip when upset.

Still he was not ready to believe it. He needed more time to think about what Jenny had told him, time to work it all through in his mind. What he needed most was to get her out of there, to give himself some breathing room. But sensing that Jenny would prove to be every bit as stubborn as his mother could be at times, he knew of only one way to go about getting her to leave, and that was to give in to her demands—or at least let her think he had.

"Tell you what," he said, his tone softening, as if suddenly inclined to compromise. "I'm willing to let Dr. Weathers decide what to do about this. He's her doctor. He'll know if she's up to the shock of having a long-lost daughter suddenly reappear in her life or not." He tried not to look too smug, certain Dr. Weathers would do whatever he could to protect his patient from someone as pushy as this Jenny Ryan. "Is that agreeable to you?"

"Yes, it is most agreeable," she said, using the same condescending tone he had used. "Besides, I am not out to cause her any harm and if it would be too much of a strain on her right now I am willing to wait until she feels better." Even if it meant she was never allowed to actually talk with her natural mother, it was better than to take a chance of her condition worsening.

Having gotten Jenny to agree to his plan, Rick lifted the receiver and immediately punched in the appropriate telephone number.

"Hello, Mrs. Weathers?" he spoke only seconds later. "This is Rick Anderson. Has your husband made it home yet?" There was a short pause, followed by, "Good, would you tell him I'd like to speak with him for a moment? Yes, it does concern Mother. No, I'm still at home. Thank you. I will."

Jenny stood frozen and weak-kneed while she waited for him to speak with the doctor. So much depended on what that doctor had to say. Her pounding heart climbed slowly into her throat while she waited for Rick's next words.

"Oh, hi, Doc. Sorry to disturb your supper, but something has come up that needs your immediate attention. No, I'm at home." He ran his tongue over his lips impatiently while he listened to something the doctor had to say. "No, it's nothing like that. It's a problem that has arisen right here at home. Well, to tell you the truth, there's a young woman over here who claims to be Mother's real daughter. She even has a birth certificate that says as much, though I don't know enough about such documents to know if it is legal or not. What? No, that won't be necessary. I just—Well, yes, but—"

Rick pulled the receiver several inches away from his ear and looked at it questioningly.

"What is it? What did he say?" she wanted to know, unable to bear the suspense any longer.

"He's coming right over." Rick looked all the more perplexed. "He said for you to wait right here."

"How far away does he live?" Jenny asked, wondering how long it would take. At the rate her heart was now pumping, she was not sure she could stand having to wait much longer.

"About three blocks," Rick told her. "He should be here within minutes."

And he was. Within a very few minutes the doctor had knocked at the front door, then promptly let himself in. As soon as he had called out to announce his arrival, Rick shouted for him to join them in the front room.

Seconds later a short man with a thinning shock of silvery gray hair entered the room, his green eyes round with expectation. He immediately focused his attention on Jenny, then came to a dead stop in the center of the room. His eyes widened, as if in some way he had recognized her.

Jenny's heart froze in mid-beat, aware of what his actions indicated, but too afraid to hope it could be true. She remained on tenterhooks while she waited for him to speak.

"That's her," Rick stated as if he felt something needed to be said to start a conversation.

"I would have known her anywhere," the doctor responded, blinking hard and adjusting his eyeglasses as if that might in some way alter what he saw. He took a tiny step closer. "She looks just like Liz did at that age."

Tears of joy filled Jenny's eyes. That was exactly the sort of thing she wanted to hear. "Do I? Do I really look like her?"

"Yes, you do," he admitted, shaking his head with disbelief while he continued to stare at her with open fascination. "It's truly amazing. It's like turning back the clock." He blinked harder still. "I can't believe you've managed to find her after all these years."

"Then you knew that Mother had had a baby?" Rick asked, his voice vibrating with all the hurt and anger he felt. If the doctor knew, then why didn't he?

Dr. Weathers turned to face him, pulling his gaze off Jenny for the first time since having entered the room. "Yes, Rick. I've known for years. Because I am as much your mother's friend as her family doctor, I've had to help her through several bouts of depression that resulted from having been forced to give up her first child."

"She was depressed because of it?" Jenny wanted to know, both touched and heartsick all at the same time. Her mother had been *forced* to give her up. She could hardly wait to hear the whole story.

"Yes," he answered her. "For several years just before Christmas, right about the time your birthday would roll around, Liz would suffer severe bouts of depression. She would sit and cry for hours, grieving the loss of her child. To her, having been forced to give up her firstborn was like having suffered a death. True, she knew you were out there somewhere, or at least she hoped you were still out there, but you were unavailable to her. She could not hold you, could not know if you were growing up happy or if you had been forced into a miserable existence.''

"I was happy. I was incredibly happy," Jenny put in, swallowing back the constriction tightening around the base of her throat. "My adoptive parents were wonderful people."

"But she had no way of knowing that, so she would worry about what she had done and would become deeply depressed. Doyal and I did everything we could to bring her out of it, but sometimes there was nothing anyone could do. She'd just have to cry it out. You see, she never really wanted to give you up. It was something her father had arranged and she went through with it because she loved him. But she often regretted it, and she has so worried about the sort of life you were forced to lead. She worried that you may have been neglected or abused.''

Jenny blinked back the tears that had collected at the outer corners of her eyes. Though it broke her heart to hear about her mother's suffering, she was filled with joy to know of her love. "Then do you think it would be all right for me to see her? To let her know that I was neither abused nor neglected? That I actually had a very happy childhood?''

"All right?" he repeated, grinning broadly, clearly excited over the prospect. "I think that might be just what she needs about now." His happy expression dropped as suddenly as it had formed, when he glanced back at Rick and saw the hurt and confusion on his face. "That is, if Rick doesn't mind."

"He's already said we would leave that decision up to you," she said, not wanting to give Rick an opportunity to change his mind. "That's why he wanted to talk to you about this in the first place."

"Then, I say, let's do it." The doctor rubbed his hands together in eager anticipation. "First thing tomorrow." He turned to Rick again. "Can you take a few hours off in the morning? I really think she'd want you to be there for this."

For the first time since hearing Dr. Weathers verify that his mother had indeed had a baby in her youth, Rick spoke, but his voice came out strained with emotion. Although it did not shock him that his mother had had a child out of wedlock, it did hurt to know she had kept it a secret from him all these years. "If you think it's what's best for Mother."

"Oh, I do. I do. Just knowing that Jenny, here, is alive and happy will put your mother's mind to rest. She has always wondered, always worried. Finding her daughter will take her mind away from her pain. It'll be better medicine than anything I could ever prescribe for her."

"Well, if you really believe that," Rick said, disgruntled that the doctor had sided with Jenny. But being a man of his word, he planned to abide by the doctor's decision no matter how much he disagreed with it. "I'll do whatever you say."

Reluctantly he listened while Dr. Weathers formulated his plan.

"I think the best thing would be to introduce them as soon as possible," he continued, dividing his attention between the two. "But I don't think tonight would be a good idea. She'd never be able to get any rest after such excitement. Besides, the last visiting period is at nine and it's almost that now. I wouldn't have time to check her first. No, I think tomorrow morning would probably be better. Liz always seems far more lucid and in much better spirits during the morning hours.''

Jenny listened intently, though what she really wanted to do was ask him exactly what was wrong with her mother, what sort of pain she was in and how serious was her illness. But she was afraid she might frighten the doctor into thinking he had made the wrong decision, that she planned to interfere in some way.

She was certain she would discover all about her mother's condition in due time. She simply would have to accept whatever bits and pieces of information were revealed to her without having to question anyone.

''What time in the morning?'' Rick wanted to know.

Twisting his face, deep in thought, Dr. Weathers gave that his full consideration. ''I'm not sure. Probably about ten. Tell you what, I'll give you a call and let you know the exact time early tomorrow morning, right after I've finished my morning examination. I'll know more about the situation after I've had a chance to talk with her. You two just sit by that phone and be ready to come on as soon as I call.'' He gestured toward the same telephone Rick had used to call him earlier.

Jenny glanced uncomfortably at Rick, aware the doctor had for some reason assumed she was staying there—with Rick and his family. ''I don't know that I'll—'' she started to explain only to be cut short by Rick.

"We'll be ready to leave the second we get your call. I'll see that we have an early breakfast."

"I can hardly wait," the doctor said, sounding as excited as a young child on Christmas Eve. "In fact, if I haven't called by nine forty-five, come on down. Chances are I will have gotten tied up with something else, but I feel certain I'll want to do this during the regular morning visiting period. Ten o'clock."

Finding his enthusiasm contagious, Jenny smiled. "That suits me fine."

"What about you?" Dr. Weathers asked Rick, who was not nearly as affected by his enthusiasm as Jenny had been. "Does that suit your plans?"

Rick hesitated, then shrugged. "Whatever you want to do is fine with me."

But it was obvious by his grim expression that he was not being totally honest. Jenny wondered about that. She wondered why he seemed so terribly upset over the doctor's decision to let them meet—then realized the reason. He felt threatened.

She should have known that would be the way he felt, especially after she had discovered he was adopted. She tried to think of something she could say to reassure him, but wasn't really sure what it was she should reassure him about. That his mother would still love him? That seemed rather obvious. Nothing Jenny could do would ever change the sort of love those two shared. Maybe she needed to reassure him again that she was not out to cause anyone any harm—not him and especially not her mother. All she wanted to do was meet the woman who had given birth to her. Surely, being an adoptee himself, he could understand that.

"Rick?" she started to say, still not certain where her words would take her.

"In a minute," he interrupted, gesturing toward the doctor. "So, you think we should just go on down there a little before ten."

Dr. Weathers nodded, rubbing his wrinkled forehead with the tips of his fingers. "Yes, I think that will probably be the best time. Speaking of time—" he glanced at his watch "—I'd better get on back to the house before Christine tosses my supper right out the window. I'll talk to you two tomorrow morning."

"I'll walk you to the door," Rick volunteered, then turned to Jenny with his hand outstretched. "Give me your keys so I can get your things while I'm out there and bring them inside."

"You don't have to do that," she commented, aware she was not exactly his favorite choice of a houseguest. "You don't have to offer me lodging."

He looked at her, exasperated by the delay. "Do you already have a place to stay?"

"Well, no, but—"

"Then give me your keys. I'll bring in your suitcases and anything else you think you'll need. You're staying here."

It was not the friendliest invitation she had ever had, but when faced with the truth like that, she had to admit she really did not have a place to stay yet, and as late as it had gotten to be she might have a hard time finding one. Reluctantly she dug into her purse for her keys. "Would you do one other favor for me?"

His eyebrows lowered, as if unable to believe she would have the audacity to ask a favor of him. "And what might that be?"

"Would you park my car somewhere besides in the street?"

A malevolent grin flickered across his face, as if he had briefly considered just where he would like to park the thing, but when he responded his voice revealed none of what had crossed his mind. The words he spoke next sounded vaguely familiar.

"Okay, fine."

When he turned away, Jenny was reminded of a very troubled thirteen-year-old girl who had stormed up the stairs barely half an hour earlier. She wondered what Rachel would have to say when she learned they were about to have an unwanted houseguest, one who had obviously caused them to miss their last opportunity to visit the hospital that day. She also wondered what Rick's wife would have to say about her being there.

Plenty, she bet. On both counts.

Chapter Four

"Are these two suitcases it?" Rick asked, when he stepped into the room several minutes later carrying one large suitcase in each hand. Although the weight of them had strained Jenny's arms when she had carried them from her house to the car earlier, he held them as if they weighed very little.

"Yes, that's all I brought."

"Well, then, we might as well get you settled in," he said, turning back toward the hall. "Since it's already five minutes till nine, there's not much point in trying to make that last visiting period. By the time Rachel and I drove over there and found a place to park, it would be too late. Those people are very strict about abiding by their posted visiting hours. I will give the ICU a call to find out how she's doing."

"I'm sorry," Jenny said, hurrying to catch up with him in the hallway. "I never meant to cause you or your family such inconvenience. I just want to meet my biological mother, is all. Surely, being adopted yourself, you can understand that."

"And it looks like you're about to get the opportunity to do just that." He still sounded somewhat annoyed over having had so little say in the matter, but not quite as embittered as he had seemed while the doctor was still there.

Rather than continue with a conversation that might lead to yet more ill feeling between them, Jenny decided to redirect the conversation onto something else. Curious to know more about her adopted half brother and his family, she asked, "I wonder what your wife will have to say when she finds out you have invited someone to stay the night, without having talked it over with her first." She shook her head while she thought about that. "I know if my ex-husband had suddenly invited someone we didn't even know to stay the night, I'd have had a few things to say about it."

"No doubt," he replied, glancing at her while he registered the fact she had an *ex*-husband. He wondered, then, if she might also have a *present* husband, but realized she would have used him for her example instead. He coupled that fact with the memory she wore no wedding ring and concluded she was presently unmarried. While he led her up the wide carpeted stairs, toward the closest, most convenient guest room, he wondered if she had any children as a result of her failed marriage but decided that was something he shouldn't ask, at least not yet. He didn't want to appear overly curious. "As used to getting your way as you seem to be, I imagine you would indeed have plenty to say."

Jenny tried not to let that remark bother her. "As I imagine your wife will. Unless of course you were lucky enough to marry a genuine saint." Somehow she doubted a man like Rick had a saintly wife. The woman could have started out saintly enough, but

Jenny knew from personal experience how trying a man such as Rick could be to even the saintliest of women. "Is that what you did? Married a saint?"

Rick's mouth flattened into a grim line. The mere thought of comparing Carla to a saint caused him to let out a short, disgusted breath. "Not only is the woman I married not a saint, she's no longer my wife. I am also divorced."

For some reason that surprised but also pleased Jenny. "How long have you been divorced?"

He looked at her, a little taken aback by how quick she was to ask such personal questions. He decided, if she had no qualms about asking such questions, then neither should he. "A little over a year. And you?"

"About that long. My husband left me last April and by the end of July the divorce was final."

Rick looked at her with amazement. "Must have been uncontested. My divorce took seven long months."

"Yes, our divorce was uncontested. I personally saw no reason to fight it. He had already found someone younger and prettier to replace me, and because he was eager to start his new life with his new lady love, he proved quite willing to divide everything we owned equally. And of course there were no children to complicate matters."

Although Rick could not imagine her ex-husband being able to find anyone more attractive than Jenny, her last comment had answered his question about any children. He wondered how long she and her ex had been married, in all. "Well, not only did I have Rachel to consider, I had a wife who wanted everything she could possibly get her hands on—whether she deserved it or not."

Jenny decided by his angry tone that the woman must have succeeded, at least in part. Having already seen some of what Rick still had, which was considerable, she wondered what all his ex-wife had ended up taking with her. Jenny guessed the woman had to be pretty well set for life.

"Then Rachel is just here for a visit?"

"No, Rachel lives with me. Our daughter was about the only thing from our marriage my wife did not want, and it is just as well, because I would have fought Carla for custody anyway, and I'd have won."

When Jenny saw the angry determination glimmering in Rick's eyes, she wondered why he felt so strongly about being the custodial parent, when it appeared he and his daughter had such a troubled relationship. "I gather Rachel is your only child."

"Unfortunately, yes."

Jenny wondered what he had meant by *unfortunately*. Did he regret not having had more children while he'd had the chance, or did he regret ever having had the one? While she looked at him, trying to decide which was true, he veered into a nearby room and she could no longer see his face.

But having turned his back to her had certainly presented her with a nice view of his wide shoulders and lean, muscular hips, which were tantalizingly displayed beneath a pair of soft, faded jeans. Suddenly she felt uncomfortable entering a bedroom alone with him.

Although they were obviously not blood-related as she had first thought, they were still just one step away from being half brother and half sister, therefore she was bewildered by the natural attraction she felt toward him. There was something morally wrong in finding him so appealing.

"This is the nicest guest room we have," he said, turning to look back at her before he set the two suitcases in the center of a very large bedroom decorated with dusty pinks and royal blues. "It is also the only one with its own bathroom. The other guest room is at the far end of the hall. It would be all right except that it shares a bathroom with Rachel, and believe me, sharing a bathroom with that girl is something I would not wish on anyone."

Jenny chuckled, knowing how messy and territorial thirteen-year-olds could be. "Thank you, I appreciate the consideration." She then glanced around at her new surroundings, pleased but not too surprised to find them furnished with such elegance. Not only was there a beautiful antique four-poster with an ivory crocheted bedspread and an elaborately carved wooden headboard, there was an extensive matching bedroom suite, including a vanity and an antique washstand. There was also a small reading area near a large set of three windows that included a small footed table and two rococo chairs.

Having always appreciated antiques as well as lots of breathing space, she could not have asked for nicer accommodations. "This room is perfect."

While she continued to scan her surroundings more closely, she noticed Rick stood facing her with a curious expression, as if he wanted to ask her something. But in the end all he did was tell her where she would find some of the items she might need during her stay.

He explained that breakfast was usually served at seven o'clock because he normally left the house around seven-thirty.

"I'll be sure to tell Jacqueline that we'll be having a guest for breakfast. How do you like your eggs?"

Jenny decided Jacqueline must be his housekeeper, because if he'd had a live-in girlfriend she felt certain he would have mentioned her by now—especially after all the other bits of information he had been so willing to impart. "Scrambled is fine."

"Then scrambled it shall be," he commented and paused to look at her one last time, as if he still wasn't quite certain what to think of her before finally leaving.

Although Jenny had expected sleep to be impossible after having experienced such an emotionally eventful day, she surprised herself by falling off to sleep almost immediately. Had she not remembered to set the small alarm clock beside her bed, she might have slept halfway through the morning. Because she became immediately alert to where she was and why, she did not have any difficulty coming awake. Nor did she linger in bed, which she normally might have done.

Aware she was now only hours away from finally meeting her birth mother, she felt immediately energetic and hurried to shower and dress.

Still wanting to make the very best first impression possible, she spent a lot of time selecting exactly what she wanted to wear. Having already worn her most flattering dress, one that accentuated both her narrow waist and the gentle flare of her hips, Jenny chose another dress she felt looked almost as flattering—a belted red percale with an open collar, where she quickly tucked the ends of a multicolored silk scarf. She next put on her usual makeup and brushed her hair until the front feathered smoothly away from her face. She then applied a light touch of hair spray to hold it in place.

When she felt certain she looked her very best, and knowing seven o'clock was rapidly approaching, she quickly made her bed, then returned her scattered belongings to her suitcases and closed them so they could be easily returned to her car.

Remembering that Rick had not seemed at all comfortable with having her there, and having no intention of leaving Tyler right away, she had decided to find somewhere else to stay, but not until they had returned from the hospital.

A shiver of anticipation rushed over Jenny when she considered what was to happen in the hours ahead. A part of her was terrified over the thought of finally meeting the woman who'd given her life, terrified she might disappoint her in some way. Still another part of her could hardly wait, especially now that she had reason to believe the woman would not send her away without having first answered a few of her many questions.

If what Dr. Weathers had indicated was true, her birth mother would be glad to see her and would probably talk with her. She would finally have the opportunity to find out the circumstances that had led to her being adopted.

Dr. Weathers had said Elizabeth had been forced to give her baby away and he had indicated that it was her father's doing, but he had not explained why. Although Jenny already knew a lot more than she had when she first arrived, there was still so very much to learn. The realization that the deep void she'd lived with all her life might soon be filled caused her heart to race with such overpowering anticipation, it created a hard, throbbing ache deep in her chest.

When Jenny entered the dining room at precisely seven o'clock she found Rick already seated at the table, reading the newspaper. There were three places set around one end of a dining table large enough to seat eight comfortably. Rick sat at the far end, facing the door, with his back to an elaborately designed china cabinet and a small buffet where a steaming pot of coffee sat warming on a small heating element.

The other two place settings were directly in front of him, one at either side, and between the other two place settings was a footed tray with two types of jelly, a small dish of butter and the salt and pepper shakers. Beside the tray was a small glass pitcher half filled with orange juice.

"Which place is mine?" she asked when he did not immediately notice she had entered.

Surprised to find her already in the room, Rick quickly folded the newspaper and stood. He indicated the chair to his right by pulling it out several inches, then set the newspaper aside. "You'll be sitting here, facing Rachel—if she ever comes down. This being her first day of summer vacation, she will probably choose to sleep late."

"I don't blame her," Jenny said as she hurried around the table to take the seat he had indicated. Although she normally felt at ease with strangers, her stomach knotted at the thought of being alone with Rick during breakfast.

She was not sure why she felt such a profound discomfort around him, but eventually decided it was because his opinion and support were so important. He would undoubtedly have a great measure of influence over their mother, and Jenny knew it would help their initial meeting run far more smoothly if he found some reason to support her in her cause.

"I know if I were still home, I'd be sleeping late," she continued as she pulled the chair farther away from the table. Her casual motions betrayed none of the painful turmoil twisting inside her when she settled into her chair. "I usually sleep fairly late on my first day of summer vacation. I feel like it should be my reward for having managed to keep hold of my sanity during the entire previous nine months."

"Oh? Are you a teacher?" he asked, looking at her as if that had been the last thing he would have expected her to be.

"Although I have taught high-school English from time to time, mainly as a substitute, I'm really more of a counselor." She took her dark blue napkin and spread it across her lap. "And have been for nearly seven years."

"Then you must have far more patience than I ever thought of having," he commented, aware it was the type of job that would send him right over the edge. "How many students in your school?"

"Stockfield has a rather small high school. This year it had just under four hundred students enrolled," she answered with a distant yet sad expression. She already missed the ninety-one seniors and hated having missed graduation. It would have been her last chance to tell them all goodbye and wish them well. "But it suits me fine to have so few students, because the lower the number, the more time I can devote to each."

"And I can't even handle my one," Rick muttered while he, too, placed his napkin in his lap. He then looked into her wide, innocent-looking brown eyes and wondered if any of her high-school students ever tried to run over her the way Rachel tried to run over him. He imagined they did, because most kids liked to find out exactly what their limits were, but he decided Jenny was the type who could handle whatever trouble they tried to give her. Remembering how easily she had handled Dr. Weathers the night before, he was certain Jenny normally came out on top whenever one of her students tried to outmaneuver her.

"Yes, Rachel did seem like she could be a handful," Jenny agreed, putting it as politely as she knew how. If there was one thing she had learned as a high-school counselor, it was that diplomacy was extremely important. "I'm curious. What did she have to say about me?"

"Not much," he admitted. "But then I didn't go into much detail when telling her about you. Because of the ticklish situation your being here has created, as well as the fact Rachel already has a lot of personal problems to cope with at the moment, about all I ended up telling her was that you were a close friend of her grandmother's and because you were such a close friend of Mother's I had invited you to stay here for a few days."

"Oh, but that won't be necessary," Jenny quickly explained. "Although I appreciate you letting me stay here last night, I have no intention of imposing on you any longer. As soon as we return from the hospital, I plan to find somewhere else to stay."

Rick shook his head as if unable to believe her naiveté. "Once Mother has found out who you are, she will demand you either remain right here with us or that you stay at her house. She's not about to let you run off to some hotel. And since you are already settled into our guest room, I see no reason for you to move."

Truth was, he was starting to like the idea of having her for a houseguest during the next few days. It was rather nice to be able to hold a conversation with an intelligent adult first thing in the morning. The most he could expect from Rachel during breakfast were one-syllable responses and a few grunts or groans. Rachel was definitely not a morning person.

"But what will people say about a single woman living in the same house with a single man, even if we are practically brother and sister?"

"We are hardly what you would call blood kin," he commented. "But you forgot to mention the pertinent fact that there will also be a teenage daughter and a fifty-year-old housekeeper living here, too," he commented then curled his mouth into a slightly perverse smile. "Besides, you staying here with us is not going to start the tongues to wagging around here nearly as much as the knowledge that you are my mother's illegitimate daughter."

Jenny met his gaze, her expression filled with concern. "That never has to come out. As far as the rest of the world is concerned, I don't have to be presented as anything more than a friend of the family."

"Maybe so," Rick said with a troubled shake of his head. "But I'm not so sure that's the way Mother will want to handle it. She quit bending her own values to accommodate propriety years ago."

Jenny tried for what had to be the thousandth time to picture the woman who had given life to her. "How do you think she will react when either you or Dr. Weathers introduces me to her as her long-lost daughter?"

Rick thought about that for a moment while pouring himself a fourth small glassful of orange juice. "I'm not really sure. Because she has never bothered to tell me about you, I have no way to know how or what she feels about you. But if what Dr. Weathers says is true, and I have no reason to doubt the man, I think she'll probably be delighted if not downright relieved to meet you." His brow drew into a contemplative frown. "But then again, there has to be a very strong reason she has kept your existence a secret all these years, and that could play heavily into her initial reaction."

"I imagine she kept me a secret because she was a little ashamed for having allowed something like that to happen," Jenny suggested, having always believed that to be the truth. "After all, she was obviously not married to the man, whoever he was."

"You could be right," Rick said, nodding reflectively and wondering for the first time who had fathered Jenny. Was it someone he knew?

Last night it had been complicated enough to try to come to terms with the startling fact his mother had given birth to a baby girl so many years ago and had then managed to keep the fact a deep, dark secret.

Now that he was finally over the shock of having had his mother's past sprung on him like that, he was curious to know more.

"Then you don't know who your father was?" While he slowly sipped his orange juice, he wondered what it must be like not knowing who your parents are. Having been adopted at the age of four, shortly after his mother's death, he at least knew whose blood ran through his veins. He knew who he'd been before he became an Anderson and knew what sort of people they were.

"Not yet," Jenny admitted. "At the moment, all I know about him is what little was on my de-identified birth records."

"Your what?"

"My de-identified birth records," she repeated, then explained. "You see, unless an adoptee has a court order releasing his or her complete records, the only information she can be given from inside her birth file is that which in no way can identify any person or place involved. Why, they even take out the parents' and grandparents' birth dates and places of birth."

"What's really left?"

"Information such as my parents' coloring, heights and weights, and any family medical history known as of the date I was born. That sort of thing. What the state does whenever they get a written request for information is photocopy an adoptee's complete records—if it's the state that even has them—then they proceed to take a razor and carefully cut out every bit of identifying information they can find, even nurses' and doctors' names. When the requested record finally is mailed out, it looks a lot like Swiss cheese.''

"How did you ever find out you could obtain these records?''

"I wrote to the National Committee for Adoption in Washington, D.C. after having gotten the address out of an old Ann Landers column and was sent a listing of addresses to contact in the states that allow such records to be mailed out. Luckily Texas was one of them.''

"But how did you come up with my mother's identity if the records you were sent had no names? And how'd you ever get a hold of your original birth certificate?''

"It's a long, complicated story," Jenny said. "But what it narrows down to is that I did eventually get my hands on my original birth certificate and that was where I found my birth mother's name. But I have yet to learn my birth father's name, since he obviously did not agree to have his name listed. I'm hoping your mother will be able to tell me a little about him—that is if she's not too embarrassed to talk about him with me.''

"I don't see why she should be all that embarrassed," Rick said as he set his glass back down to refill it yet again. "Everyone makes mistakes, some are just a little more serious than others.''

Not wanting the conversation to remain on such a somber level, especially when her insides were already in such a frantic state of turmoil that she could hardly breathe, Jenny decided it was time to lighten the mood a little. "Are you now insinuating that I was some sort of serious mistake?''

Aware of the playfulness in her tone of voice and that what he had said did indeed sound as if that's what he had meant, Rick chuckled. "Well, if the shoe fits—"

"I'll have you know that is one shoe I refuse to even try on," she retorted, encouraged by how easily they were able to tease one another. She might win his support yet.

At that moment the swinging door behind Jenny was pushed open. She turned in time to see a short, stocky older woman wearing a starched white apron over a crisp blue uniform enter the dining room. Smiling cheerfully when she stepped into the room, she appeared very neat and proper. She wore her hair in a long sandy-colored braid in a wide double loop at the top of her head.

"Good mornin'," she said in a soft, drawling accent that reminded Jenny of her Aunt Shirley from Alabama. "I have your eggs, biscuits and ham all ready. I sure hope y'all are hungry." She wasted little time setting the two plates she carried in front of them, then glanced around at the different items on the table. "Anything else?"

"Just more orange juice," Rick said, indicating the small pitcher on the table, which by now was nearly empty. "I seem to be a little thirstier than usual."

When the housekeeper returned moments later with the refilled pitcher, Jenny noticed the way she kept staring at her as if trying to recognize her.

"So you're a friend of Mrs. Anderson's?" she asked, while she busied herself checking the condiments on the table, making sure there was enough of everything.

When Jenny glanced at Rick and noticed his brisk, indicative nod, she realized that was the story he had decided to tell everyone. "Yes, I am. Although I'll admit I haven't seen her in quite some time."

Rick fought the urge to grin at such an honest, yet blatantly misleading answer.

"And you're going with Mr. Rick to the hospital to see her this morning?"

"I certainly hope to." Jenny wondered why all the questions.

"Good. Tell her Rosetta and I said for her to hurry up and get better. We are past ready for her to get herself out of there so we can take care of her good and proper," she explained, clucking her tongue with dismay. "A hospital is no place for a sick person."

Jenny's eyebrows arched, wondering where the woman had obtained such a poor opinion of hospitals. "I'll be sure and tell her that."

"Jacqueline believes that the only two people who can possibly care for Mother properly are Mother's housekeeper and of course Jacqueline herself," Rick explained. "All those doctors and nurses with their years of training and experience don't mean anything to her."

"That's because Rosetta and I can do a far sight better job of taking care of her than those stern-faced nurses and doctors do," Jacqueline protested, tossing her nose in the air and wrinkling her face to show exactly what she thought of the medical profession as a whole. "Takes lots of good old loving care to make a person finally get well." She then looked at Rick after another thought had occurred to her. "Is Rachel supposed to be going with y'all? If so, I'd better see what I can do about getting her up.''

"Don't bother. There can only be two people each visitation, and I'm planning to go in with Jenny. Rachel will just have to wait until two o'clock.''

"If she's even awake by then," Jacqueline muttered just before she headed for the kitchen again. "That girl can sleep longer than anybody I ever met.''

Jenny waited until the door had swung shut behind the woman before she turned to face Rick, concerned to learn she would be bumping Rachel from her normal visiting time. "I hope your daughter won't become too upset with me for having taken her place this morning. I'd hate to get off on the wrong foot with her.''

"It won't matter much to Rachel, as long as I let her go this afternoon. Besides, Jacqueline was right. If left alone, Rachel will undoubtedly sleep right through to lunch. Now eat your breakfast before it gets cold,'' he said, indicating the food on her plate, which she had yet to touch. "At the rate you're going it'll take you all day to finish that one plate of food. I plan for us to leave here shortly after nine.''

Chapter Five

Jenny's heart pounded with such painful magnitude during the short ride to the hospital that she feared she would never survive the onslaught. With each new building or street they passed, with each block closer they drove, her heartbeat accelerated just that much more, aware she was that much closer to finally meeting her birth mother.

When she noticed the convenience store where she had stopped the day before to buy a map of the city, she knew they were now only minutes away. Minutes away from finding out whether Elizabeth Ellen Thornton, now Elizabeth Ellen Anderson, would willingly accept her back into her life—if only for the next few days. Or whether she would cast her aside yet again.

Although Jenny had known from the beginning that what she had set out to do could very well end with another painful rejection, and had been fully aware of the deep emotional risk involved, she was suddenly not all that certain she could handle yet another rejection—especially if that rejection was to come from the very woman who had given her life.

It had been painful enough to discover that after ten years of what she thought was a perfectly good marriage her own husband had suddenly decided he wanted her out of his life and had promptly tossed her aside like yesterday's newspaper. To now be similarly rejected by her own biological mother could prove devastating.

What she needed at this point in her life was to be accepted again, to be told that her birth mother had indeed given her up because of circumstances beyond her control and not because she had simply decided she did not want her.

But even if the latter turned out to be the case, even if she had been adopted out for convenience' sake, Jenny was ready to accept the truth. No matter how painful that truth might be, Jenny had to fill the deep, hollow void that had always existed in her life—the strange feeling of emptiness that resulted simply from not knowing.

No matter what the eventual outcome, at least she would finally know the truth and could put that portion of her life to rest. She would have finally fulfilled her quest to know, and that in itself would be reward enough.

When Rick brought his dark blue Trofeo to a halt in a parking spot that had just been vacated a few feet from the front door of the hospital, Jenny took several deep, sustaining breaths before reaching for the door handle. She could not remember ever having felt so apprehensive about anything in her entire life and again wondered if she had the stamina to actually go through with it. As badly as she wanted to learn more about herself, and as badly as she wanted to know something about the woman who had given birth to her, she was not so sure her heart could take the strain. It pounded with such force now, she felt ravaged inside.

"Ready?" Rick asked after he had opened the door for her and stepped back to give her room.

"As I'll ever be," she muttered, her eyes stretched so wide with trepidation she doubted she could blink even if she wanted. When she stepped out of the car and turned to look into his discerning blue eyes, she noticed her legs felt a little weak yet remained surprisingly steady. Brushing the wrinkles from her skirt, she wondered what was going through Rick's mind at that moment. Was he still against the idea, or had he started to understand why it was so important to her?

"Then let's go find Dr. Weathers and let him know we are here," he said with a slight forward movement of his hand, giving no indication what his feelings might be. When she did not immediately respond, he smiled reassuringly. "Time's a-wasting."

Jenny studied his expression a few seconds longer before finally returning his smile. She held the smile when she turned in the direction he had indicated and headed toward the building.

She was relieved to know Rick had somehow come to terms with who she was and why she was there. All the anger and resentment he had shown the evening before were now gone. In their place was a sort of quiet reserve.

"What time is it?" Jenny asked, wrapping her hand around the portion of her wrist where her watch should have been. Although she had noticed the hour when they first left the house, she had lost track of the time during the short side trip by the large auto parts warehouse where Rick worked.

Not having planned to take the day off, Rick had had a few quick matters to take care of before going on to the hospital. Although Jenny had not asked, for fear she would not be able to give his answer the attention it might need, she suspected he either owned or managed the warehouse because of the way the employees who had been outside unloading a large truck had hurried their pace when they spotted him getting out of his car.

"It's about nine forty-five," Rick answered without glancing at his watch. He was obviously not quite as distracted as Jenny. "That should give us just enough time to have a short talk with Dr. Weathers and find out exactly how he wants us to handle this before actually going in to see Mother."

Jenny drew in a deep breath and held it until they finally reached the promenade then exhaled softly before she turned to look at Rick with genuine amazement. "I'm really going to meet her, aren't I?"

It seemed too phenomenal to be true.

Rick studied the powerful emotions crossing her face, then smiled, aware just how important this was for her. Although he still had a few doubts plaguing him, he would not try to stop the two from meeting. Instead he followed Jenny on inside, walking beside her when she headed down the first corridor.

For several seconds after they had entered the building and turned to the right, all that could be heard was the soft chime of the elevators off to one side and the rapid click of Jenny's heels against the gray tiled floor.

"Something tells me you've been here before," Rick commented, having noticed she had not turned to him for direction.

Jenny looked at him apologetically. She should have mentioned her trip by there the afternoon before. "You're right. I have been here before. I came by yesterday wanting to find out something about her illness."

"So that's why you never bothered to ask me what's wrong with Mother. You already knew."

When Jenny turned down the second corridor that eventually led to the intensive-care unit, she felt her heart rate double. It was awfully hard for her to concentrate on their conversation, knowing only a few hundred yards ahead was the final turn that entered right into the ICU area.

She moistened her lips with the tip of her tongue before responding to his last statement. "No, I have no idea what's wrong with her. Because I didn't think it was my right to come in here and suddenly announce myself as family, they refused to tell me anything."

She looked at him, her brown eyes enormous with dread. "The truth is, I've been afraid to ask. I was afraid I'd be told her illness is terminal. I don't think I could handle knowing that just yet."

Able to see how truly frightened she was, Rick chose his next words very carefully. "Her condition is obviously very serious or she would not be in ICU, and there have been a few times when we wondered if she would make it through the night, but most of the worst danger is over." He smiled as a way to cheer her. "Otherwise Dr. Weathers would never have suggested you come here today."

Jenny thought about that and decided what he said made sense. Dr. Weathers did not seem like the type of doctor who would run any unnecessary risks where his patients were concerned. By the time they had arrived at the small nurses' station near ICU, she had put that worry behind her, but had promptly replaced it with all her earlier worries concerning what might happen when she and her birth mother finally met.

"I wonder where everyone is," Rick remarked when he noticed all six chairs in the nurses' station were empty. He then glanced down the two short hallways that branched off from the station at right angles and saw no one in sight.

If it had not been for a tall mug of steaming coffee on the desk near an open file and the constant movement of the dozen or so monitors lining one wall, the place might have seemed totally abandoned.

"The nurses are probably in the rooms getting the patients ready for their visitors," Jenny offered. When she glanced at the large round clock on the wall, she noticed it was only ten minutes until time to go in.

Only ten minutes.

Taking another deep breath, she pressed both hands against her breastbone, as if that might help control the wild thudding of her heart.

"Rick." A feminine voice called out, barely heard above the clamor rising inside her.

Jenny turned in time to see "Nurse Stoneface" from the afternoon before wrap the lower portion of a black stethoscope around her neck before heading in their direction. Although the nurse's expression as a whole remained unchanged, her eyes widened when she came close enough to recognize Jenny.

"I'm afraid I have some bad news," she said, pulling her gaze off Jenny so she could look directly at Rick.

Rick was too concerned with what was about to be said to bother with introductions, but Jenny stood close enough now to read the black-and-white tag pinned above the breast pocket of her starched white uniform. Stella Sanford was a registered charge nurse.

"What sort of bad news?" Rick asked. Although his expression revealed none of the fear that had suddenly overcome him, his tone was clearly apprehensive.

"It's about your mother," she answered then purposely cast a glance at Jenny, as if to ask whether she should be allowed to hear whatever was about to be said.

"What about Mother?" Rick asked, too worried about his mother's health to consider anything else. "What happened?"

"Your mother has had a bad night. Dr. Weathers and Dr. Buller are in with her now, and Dr. Mauldin just left. About thirty minutes ago Dr. Weathers had me call your house to warn you what was going on, but you'd already left. He then asked me to keep an eye out for you and have you wait for him right here beside the nurses' station. He should be out in a few minutes. He can tell you more about what's happened." She rested her hand on Rick's shoulder briefly as if wanting to comfort him somehow. "I'll go tell him that you are here."

When Jenny glanced at Rick and saw how pale he looked, she felt a tight knot form in her chest. She noticed his unblinking gaze travel to one of the nearby glassed-in cubicles, where a large sea-green curtain had been tightly drawn and realized that must be their mother's room.

After watching Nurse Sanford slip inside and carefully close the door behind her, she knew that had to be where her mother now lay. She swallowed hard when she then noticed that the curtains in the other cubicles had remained open, the patients in clear sight of the nurses' station. Another wave of apprehension washed over her.

Something was seriously wrong.

Unable to bear the thought of losing her mother after having come that close, Jenny closed her eyes and offered a silent prayer. If God had any mercy at all, he would see that she didn't die.

"Here comes Doc Weathers," Rick said when he noticed the door open, then stepped forward to meet him halfway.

Jenny was surprised to see Dr. Weathers coming out of the small room dressed in a tan sports coat, plaid pants, a pink shirt and a bright red tie. If it was not for the stethoscope protruding from his lower front pocket, she would never have guessed him to be a doctor—a newscaster or possibly a salesman of some sort, but never a doctor.

Reluctantly she followed Rick across the corridor. She dreaded hearing what the doctor had to say, but at the same time had to know exactly how serious the situation had become.

"I'm sorry, Rick, but your mother has taken an unexpected turn for the worse," Dr. Weathers said, placing a gentle hand on Rick's shoulder to help steady him. He then looked at Jenny, who stood too far away to touch, his pale green eyes filled with compassion. "Liz has slipped into another coma."

Every muscle inside Rick stiffened visibly. "How bad is it this time?"

"You know I'm not the type to lie to you. It looks pretty bad." He then glanced at Jenny's confused expression and explained. "This is her third time to slip into a coma. But before her comas had always been the result of a sudden high fever, therefore it was generally a simple matter of getting her temperature back under control and we would be able to bring her out of her comatose state fairly quickly. This time, I'm afraid it is a little more complicated than that."

"Why?" Rick wanted to know. "What's happened?"

"It's that pancreas again. Only this time she's got more than a simple inflammation. This time the pancreas has blocked itself off entirely. If the medication Dr. Buller and I just added to her IV doesn't work to open her back up, and work quickly, her pancreas will literally eat itself alive with its own digestive juices."

"And she will die?" Rick asked, wanting to know exactly what he now faced.

"I think you should be prepared for that possibility."

The muscles in Rick's face hardened until his jaw looked distorted. "How long does she have?"

"That's hard to say. Could be days. Could be hours. Could be years. But if that pancreas doesn't open up, and soon, I really can't offer you much hope."

"If it doesn't open, will she then remain in the coma until—?" Rick's voice finally broke. He could not bring himself to speak the words aloud.

"Yes," Dr. Weathers answered, knowing what Rick had been about to say. "Actually the coma is a blessing of sorts. If your mother was awake at this point, she would be in such severe pain we would be forced to sedate her heavily with drugs, which could in turn slow down the effect of the other medication. As it is, we're able to keep her pain medication down to a minimum. Just enough to keep her from becoming restless. We do want her as comfortable as possible."

A silent scream welled up inside Jenny while she looked from the doctor's solemn expression to Rick's horror-struck features. This could not be happening. She had come there with too much hope to be now told that the woman she so longed to meet might die.

At that moment the door to her mother's room opened and out stepped a young bearded man in a white coat. He, too, had a stethoscope protruding from his lower front pocket, as well as a handful of tongue depressors jutting from his upper pocket.

Aware Jenny would not know who the younger man was, Dr. Weathers immediately introduced him. "Jenny Ryan, this is Dr. Buller, your mother's internist."

The young doctor's eyebrows shot up at the verbal indication that the patient they had just seen was also this young woman's mother, but he did not question the credibility of Dr. Weathers's remark. Instead he extended his hand for a proper handshake.

"Pleased to meet you," he responded in a quiet voice. "I guess Lowell, here, has had enough time to fill you in on what all has happened."

"I've told them everything," Dr. Weathers assured him.

"Well, I think you should also know that her heartbeat has finally stabilized and she is now resting comfortably. We've done all we can for her medically. All that's left is to wait and see if the medication we have given her will take effect in time."

Jenny appreciated his honesty, though what he said hurt her tremendously. She then looked at Dr. Weathers to see if he planned to add anything to what the younger doctor had just said.

"Jenny, I realize what a terrible disappointment this must be for you," he said, resting his free hand on her shoulder as if hoping to reassure her in much the same way he had Rick.

Disappointment?

That hardly seemed the appropriate word for the deep pain she now felt. *Devastated* would come closer to identifying the agony gripping her at that moment. She could well imagine what Rick felt.

"Tell you what," Dr. Weathers said, in a voice that sounded a little more encouraging than it had before. "Since we do have her stabilized at the moment and she is resting quietly, I think it would be all right for the two of you to go on in and see her. But only for a few minutes."

"Thank you, Doctor," Rick responded, his voice strained, then glanced again at the room where their mother lay. "We won't take long."

He pulled his hands out of the pockets of his slacks and indicated with a forward motion Jenny should go ahead of him.

"Wait just a second," Dr. Weathers said as an afterthought, his voice filled with concern. "I think I should caution Jenny about what she will see after she's in there. Even though Liz is still running a very high fever, her face is very pale, and because of the severe swelling of her pancreas, that whole area near her stomach looks enlarged. Although she is presently comatose and basically resting, she will twitch from time to time—but that is more reflex than anything else. I really don't think she is aware of the stress her body is suffering.''

"Nor will she be aware of you,'' Dr. Buller added, wanting to be sure they were not disappointed when she failed to respond to their presence.

There was a long silence while this new information was absorbed, before Rick again gestured for Jenny to go first.

Dr. Buller stepped ahead of them and pushed the door open by leaning forward from the hallway.

On knees that felt as if they would collapse at any second, Jenny entered the small room. A dull light glowed eerily from a large wall unit directly behind the bed, allowing Jenny to see everything in the room, though barely.

Tears filled her eyes when she first noticed the woman lying peacefully between stark white sheets. Nurse Sanford, who was still in the room and standing off to one side, had pulled the top sheet neatly up past her chest and had then positioned her arms on either side.

If it had not been for the plastic tubes running into both those arms and up under the sheet, Elizabeth Anderson would have looked as if she was merely sleeping and might wake up at any moment to greet them.

If only she would.

Shaking uncontrollably, aware this was the woman she'd struggled so hard to find, Jenny stepped closer. The dim light was just enough to let her see every feature of her mother's restful face. She was so enthralled by what she saw, she was only vaguely aware when the nurse stepped out of the room, gently closing the door behind her.

Jenny clenched her hands in a futile attempt to control the raw emotions tumbling inside her while she studied the woman lying before her more closely. Odd, she did not look old enough to have given birth to a baby girl over twenty-nine years ago. Yet it was obvious this was her mother. The shape of the woman's face and the color of her hair were too much like her own to leave her with any remaining doubts.

Unaware Rick had entered the room just seconds before the nurse had closed the door and now stood quietly to one side, Jenny reached out a trembling hand and touched her mother's arm ever so gently. Blinking back the resulting rush of tears, she wondered if that arm had ever held her—or had she been immediately whisked away after birth. There was so much Jenny did not know. So much that only this woman could ever tell her.

Seeing that one of her tears had dropped from her cheek and landed on the bed sheet near her mother's shoulder, Jenny reached up to dash away the excess with her trembling fingers, reminded that she was one of those people who never had a handkerchief when they needed one.

When she had wiped the tears away as best she could and had cleared her vision well enough to see again, she gazed back down into her mother's face, wishing those eyes would open so she could see what color they were.

Her birth records had claimed the eyes would be brown, but what shade? Were they dark like her own or were they a lighter brown? Did they sparkle with laughter, or were they the type to hide the emotions within?

Rick stood back watching Jenny for several seconds, aware her attention had focused on their mother's face. Able to see the emotional questions tormenting her, he stepped forward and whispered softly just inches from her ear, "Her eyes are dark brown. Just like yours."

He then put a supportive arm around her trembling shoulders and pulled her gently against him. "And when she smiles, she has the very same dimples you have."

Knowing that he was putting his own pain aside to help console her, Jenny fought the resulting maelstrom of emotions as best she could but continued to tremble violently.

After several more minutes standing beside her mother with Rick's arm still around her, steadying her, the door opened several inches and Dr. Weathers slipped inside. He glanced quickly at the different monitors about the room and then reached for Elizabeth's wrist where he held his fingertips over the pulse point for several seconds.

"Time for you to leave," he said in a voice so soft he was barely heard. "We need to run a few more lab tests on her and I'd like to get that done before those lab techs break for lunch."

He waited until Rick had led Jenny from the room, then followed them out into the corridor. When he turned to them again, he looked far more hopeful than he had before. "I certainly am glad to see that her heartbeat is so much stronger than it was. That's always a good sign."

"Let's just hope it stays that way until that medicine has had a chance to take effect," Rick commented, nodding to indicate he agreed with Dr. Weathers, though his expression remained deeply troubled. "How long until you know whether it has started to work or not?"

"Should know in the next few hours. Although we can't expect the blockage to go away immediately, I should be able to tell if the medicine is doing what it is supposed to do by sometime this afternoon. But I think I should caution you that this is that experimental drug I told you about when you first brought her in. Remember? That's why I asked you to sign those forms. I didn't want to waste any valuable time trying to find you to get your permission when the time came to use it. I knew right then that there was a very real possibility of this happening."

"But you told me you thought there would be very little risk in her taking it," Rick reminded him, worried now that he had misunderstood.

"And when you consider what will happen if she doesn't have it, the risk is indeed minimal. From everything I've read about this drug thus far, I don't think the side effects will prove any more harmful than most of the approved drugs we have today. Truth is, there may not be any side effects at all. You just can't tell about these things."

"You will call us if there's *any* change, won't you?" Rick asked, wanting to be there if and when the time came.

"You know I will," the doctor answered. "But don't sound so defeated. There's a very good chance this will work."

"We'll be at my house waiting for your call," he said, then turned to leave the ICU area before he became too emotional. He reached for Jenny's hand to be sure she followed.

Dr. Weathers walked with them as far as the next corridor.

"How long are you planning to stay in Tyler?" he asked Jenny.

"Originally I had planned to be here only a few days. But now I'm not sure how long I'll be here. I hope to stay until she's well enough to reschedule our meeting."

"Good. I hate to think of the tongue-lashing I'd get if she was to wake up and find out she had missed her chance to finally meet you. Why, she'd have my hide."

"Because I usually don't have to report back to work until the second week in July, I should have no problem arranging to stay until then. But I'd be willing to stay even longer than that if necessary," she said, then made a very real effort to smile. "Whatever it takes to save your poor hide."

Chapter Six

By the time Rick had parked the car in the garage, which was connected to the house by a short covered walkway, Jenny felt much better. During the ride home he had managed to convince her as well as himself that as long as their mother was alive and fighting, they should continue to have hope.

It had been the first time he had openly acknowledged the fact they shared the same mother, and that acknowledgment had not only caught Jenny's attention, it had given her hope that she might one day be fully accepted by her birth mother's family. He had also sounded very sincere when inviting her to stay with him and his daughter for as long as she remained in Tyler.

Clearly Rick had already accepted her as his mother's biological daughter, and that alone made Jenny feel remarkably better.

She was still dwelling on how good it felt to have Rick behave so kindly toward her, when they stepped out of the garage and headed toward the back of the house. But the peaceful mood was quickly broken when they were immediately overcome by the loud thumping of rock music.

Rick scowled while he hurried ahead of her toward the back door.

"I've told that girl to keep her music down," he muttered just loud enough to be heard over the throbbing that filled the air. When he stepped inside the house and found the noise level even more intolerable he glanced angrily in the direction of her room. With Jenny right behind him, he headed down the hall toward the closest stairs, but before he was quite halfway he also noticed a television blaring off to his left.

He glanced into the den and found not only had the television been left on at full volume, there were throw pillows scattered everywhere, a half-eaten cinnamon roll lying on one of the coffee tables, and an empty glass with a thin coating of milk standing in the midst of several wadded food wrappers on one of the end tables.

His expression became rock-hard when he stalked over to the wall intercom just inside the door, flipped a couple of switches, then shouted into the speaker.

"Rachel Leigh Anderson, turn off that stereo and get down here this instant."

When he released a lever he'd been holding, all he heard in response to his angry mandate was the loud reverberation of music. He tried again. "Rachel Leigh, I said turn off that music and get down here. *Now!*"

This time she must have heard him above the thunderous clamor of her music, because the noise lowered to a far more tolerable level seconds before her voice trickled over the speaker. "I'm coming. I'm coming."

By the time Rachel appeared in the doorway Rick was still fuming, but he managed to keep his voice low and controlled when he spoke to her. "Rachel, you know you are not supposed to play your music that loud."

"You call that loud?" came her impudent response. She crossed her arms and stared at him defiantly.

Rick curled his hands into fists in an effort not to lose his temper completely. "When I can hear it all the way outside, yes, I do call it loud. I call it very loud."

"So?" she asked, then narrowed her eyes as if daring him to say more.

"So, keep it turned down enough so that the neighbors don't have to listen to it. Also, I want you to take a good look at this room." He gestured toward the clutter on the nearest table. "Look at how messy you've left it."

Rachel glanced in the direction he had indicated, then returned her gaze to meet his, her eyelashes still low over a menacing glare. "So?"

That did it. Rick had had enough of her impudence. Angrily he reached over and turned down the television, which was still blaring, so his next words would be clearly understood.

"So clean it up!" he said through lips pressed tightly against clenched teeth so furious with her that the muscles near the back of his jaw pumped in and out in a rapid, rhythmic motion. "You are thirteen years old, for heaven's sake. You are far too old to be making these kinds of messes."

Jenny stood just inside the doorway only a few feet away from Rachel, watching apprehensively while the girl narrowed her blue eyes even further.

"Mother would never talk to me like that," she said, jutting her chin forward in a continued show of defiance.

Rick stared at her a long moment, all the while drawing in deep, barely controlled breaths. When he finally spoke again, he managed a much calmer tone. "I am not your mother. I am your father. And this is my house. And as long as you live in my house, you will follow my rules. And one of my rules happens to be that you clean up after yourself. Which you *will* do."

He again took a long, deep breath, then finished what he had to say. "I have to make a couple of important telephone calls. Your grandmother is not doing as well as she was, therefore I need to let Aunt Nicolle and Uncle Shawn know. But that should take only about ten or fifteen minutes. When I return after making those two phone calls, I had better find this room clean and that television turned off. I will see to it myself that your music is turned all the way off." He indicated the pulsating sound still coming from upstairs with an angry jerk of his head. Although it was not as loud as it had been, it could still be heard downstairs.

Jenny closed her eyes and prayed that the girl had enough sense not to press her father any further. Knowing what they had just been through at the hospital, she was certain Rick had to be very near an emotional breaking point. She was very relieved when instead of hearing an impertinent refusal to clean up her mess, all Rachel had to say on the matter was, "Okay, fine. I'll clean it up."

Rachel waited until he had left the room before wrinkling her nose and adding, "Although I don't see why Jacqueline can't clean it up when she gets back from shopping. After all, that's part of what she's paid to do."

When she then turned back around to face the mess she had made, she noticed Jenny was still in the room.

"Can you believe the way he shouted at me?" she asked, her lower lip trembling as she glanced back toward the door where she'd last seen her father.

Jenny considered pointing out the fact he had been forced to shout merely to be heard over the music and the television, but wisely she decided against it. It was too important Rachel accept her.

"Your father has had a very trying morning. Your grandmother really is worse."

Rachel's eyes widened, and for the first time since Jenny's arrival she showed genuine concern for someone besides herself. "How much worse?"

Jenny knew Rick should be the one to tell Rachel exactly how serious her grandmother's illness had become, so she chose her words carefully. "Enough that your father is planning to stay home today and wait for the doctor's telephone call."

Rachel fell momentarily silent and set about cleaning up her mess. While she gathered some of the pillows and returned them to their proper places she looked as if she might actually regret having behaved so badly, until she heard her music suddenly cut off overhead. The resentment returned to her face immediately.

"Even if Grandma is worse, that gave him no right to yell at me."

"I know. But sometimes adults do things they really don't mean to do," she said as she began helping Rachel with the mess she had made. "It's only human to react on emotions like that."

Although Jenny sensed the girl desperately needed someone to talk to and was more than willing to be that someone when the time came, she knew now was not that time. She knew from her experience as a counselor that Rachel would have to get to know her first. She would have to feel a lot more comfortable around her, comfortable enough to think of her as a friend.

With that goal in mind, Jenny then nudged Rachel playfully and added, "And contrary to what you might believe, parents are human, too."

Rachel looked at her for a long moment as if not quite sure what to make of her, then slowly grinned. "Yeah, I've heard that rumor, though I wasn't sure what to make of it."

Still grinning, she bent forward to pick the clutter off the end table, stuffing all her food wrappers and the largest of the crumbs she had scattered directly into the glass so she would have less to carry. When she finished she looked at Jenny again, this time with a raised eyebrow. "So are you a parent, too, or what?"

"No, I'm not a parent," Jenny admitted. "I was never lucky enough to have any children of my own."

Rachel continued to look at her with her head cocked to one side, as if that might help her with her initial appraisal. "Too bad. I think you'd probably make a pretty neat parent."

"Thank you," Jenny said, then indicated the sticky, half-eaten cinnamon roll she had just picked up off the coffee table and teased, "I wish I could return the compliment and say I think you make a pretty *neat* kid, but at the moment neat is not exactly the word that comes to mind."

Rachel rolled her eyes to indicate how moronic that statement had been, but laughed all the same. "You think this is bad, you should see my bedroom."

"No, thanks. I haven't had any lunch yet," Jenny said with such a straight face Rachel had to chuckle.

When Rick returned a few minutes later, he was surprised to find not only that the room was clean again but that Rachel was actually laughing. It had been months since he had heard his daughter's laughter. Although he was certain she still laughed with her friends and teammates whenever she was away from home, it was something she refused to share with him anymore. All because she still blamed him for the divorce.

"What's so funny?" he asked after he entered the room and found Rachel and Jenny fighting playfully over a cleaning rag.

"Nothing," they both answered at the same time and tried unsuccessfully to pull in their smiles to prove it.

"Why would you think anything was funny?" Jenny went on to ask, looking at him with round-eyed innocence, then winked to let him know he should go along rather than continue to question them.

"I'm not really sure. I guess it was all that snickering I heard when I first came in," he said, watching curiously while the two gave each other knowing glances. It was nice to see Rachel so happy again.

"Snickering?" Jenny asked, as if she had no idea what Rick meant. Her brow knitted into a perplexed frown. "Did you hear any snickering, Rachel?"

"Not a bit," Rachel said, still trying to straighten out her grin. "Must have come from outside somewhere."

"Yes, it was probably the neighbors," Jenny agreed with as serious an expression as she could produce at that moment, then gestured to the area around them. "So, are you pleased with the room?"

"Well, truth is, I never did care for the color of that couch," he answered, deciding to keep the mood light. "But other than that, yes, I'm very pleased with this room."

Again Rachel rolled her eyes, but rather than come back with some cutting retort as he expected, she responded with another quick laugh. "I think she meant to ask if it's clean enough to satisfy you."

Jenny nodded briskly, her brown hair bobbing past her shoulders. "Yes, that's exactly what I meant to ask. Thank you for clarifying that for me. Thank you very much."

"You're welcome very much," Rachel retorted, also nodding briskly, still unable to repress a grin.

Rick was not sure what had happened between the two while he was gone, but he was very glad it had. Still looking at them with a peculiar expression, he bent forward to run a fingertip over the shiny surface of the table.

"Yes, I do believe this table is clean enough we could eat off of it," he mused.

"Then why don't we?" Jenny asked, glancing at Rachel to see what she thought of the idea. Rachel nodded her approval.

"Why don't we what?" Rick asked, slow to catch on.

"Why don't we have lunch in here? We can follow your suggestion and eat right on this table, Japanese-style. After all, it's almost one o'clock and we haven't had anything to eat since seven." She then looked at Rachel with a raised eyebrow and corrected that comment, "Or at least *some* of us haven't had anything to eat since seven."

Rather than do anything that might spoil the moment, Rick agreed, and to his bewilderment Jenny and Rachel then hurried off to the kitchen to pack a picnic lunch.

Eating in the den proved to be just the distraction Rick needed to keep his mind off his mother. While listening to Jenny and Rachel toss jokes back and forth, he was able to concentrate solely on his daughter's laughter and on how very easily Jenny seemed to bring it out of her. Her ability to handle teenagers was astounding.

By the time they had finished their unusual meal and Jenny and Rachel had set about cleaning up, he was feeling downright lighthearted.

When Rachel went upstairs shortly after four to get ready for softball practice, Rick turned to Jenny, eager to tell her how pleased he was with all she had accomplished in such a short time, but before he could get the words out, there came an unexpected knock at the front door.

"I wonder who that could be?" Rick asked, frowning over such an untimely interruption, when he pushed himself up to answer the door. He had so wanted Jenny to know what she'd accomplished. "It's too early for Shelly or Sheila to be by for Rachel."

Something told Jenny she should follow. She was only a few feet away when Rick opened the door and discovered an extremely solemn-faced Dr. Weathers. When she noticed Rick's expression darken, she felt her heart twist with immediate apprehension. Rick knew Dr. Weathers well enough to assess his moods, and he had obviously assessed this one as extremely serious.

"I thought you were planning to call," Rick said, his expression uncertain when he stepped back to let the doctor enter.

"I was. But what I have to say is better said in person," Dr. Weathers explained, taking off his narrow-brimmed hat and tossing it onto a nearby table.

Jenny felt a tight knot form in her chest, causing her unbearable pain. It felt like her heart had been impaled on sharp spikes.

Rick looked just as troubled when he took a deep breath then gestured toward the nearest room, which was the den. "I guess we'd better sit down for this."

"Yes, I think it would be best," Dr. Weathers agreed, then followed Jenny and preceded Rick into the nearby room.

Jenny sat down on one end of the sofa and watched while the doctor sat down right beside her. She then watched while Rick slowly sank into the chair directly across from them. Although he was obviously too proud to permit his true emotions to show, she noticed his hands trembled ever so slightly when he rested them on the padded arms of the chair. That blatant refusal to display his emotions reminded Jenny of her ex-husband, Robert, who had also refused to show his deepest emotions.

Some men were simply too proud for their own good.

Dr. Weathers waited until they were all seated before starting what he had come there to say. "It's about your mother." He paused, apparently trying to decide how to word it.

"What about Mother?" Rick asked, eager to know.

A chill skipped along Jenny's spine as she steeled herself for the worst.

"I really don't know how to go about telling you," he said, his face twisting into a peculiar frown.

"Best way is to just up and say it," Rick stated, ready to get it over, unable to bear not knowing what had happened a minute longer.

When the doctor glanced at him and noticed just how emotionally strained Rick looked, he realized what must be going through Rick's mind. "Don't get the wrong idea about this. Your mother hasn't died or anything like that."

Rick's shoulders sagged with relief, but that was the only indication of the many emotions raging inside him. "Then what is it? What's wrong? Is the medicine not going to work?"

Dr. Weather's expression brightened. "Oh, but the medicine is already working. Didn't Dr. Buller's nurse call you?"

"No, no one has called us."

"Oh, I'm sorry. I thought Dr. Buller had his nurse call you earlier this afternoon. Your mother has already started showing a definite response to the medicine we gave her. She came out of her coma a little over an hour ago." He frowned then added, "But I guess she came to *after* Dr. Buller had already left, so his nurse couldn't have told you that part of it even had she called. I really should have realized that."

"Then she's out of her coma for good?" Rick asked, leaning eagerly toward him. "Her pancreas isn't blocked anymore?"

"There's still a great deal of blockage, but there is enough of an opening now that the digestive fluids are getting out. That's really all we needed to save this situation. We now have every reason to believe that your mother will have a full recovery."

"I don't understand. If Mother's pancreas is better, then why did you look so serious when you first entered?"

"Because we now have a whole different problem. Although your mother is again off the critical list and has come out of her comatose state, she seems to be suffering from a mild form of memory loss and is very confused about a lot of things."

"Memory loss?" Jenny and Rick repeated in unison.

"Yes. That's why I came by," he said, looking at Rick. "I wanted to warn you about this amnesia thing before you went in to see her again, which you and Rachel will be allowed to do this evening."

Rick's forehead knotted into a deep frown. "What caused it? Is it some sort of side effect from that experimental drug?"

"We have no way of knowing what caused it," the doctor admitted. "It may be chemically related or it may be a psychological problem. The brain is a tricky device. It can block out certain memories for years, then suddenly let them back in. No one knows why. And because this sort of thing is so complicated, I thought I'd better come over and discuss it with you personally. I wanted you to be forewarned before you talk with her."

"Forewarned? About what?" Rick asked, then his eyes widened. "Are you telling me that she's not going to recognize me? That she doesn't remember having a son?"

"I have no way of knowing what she does and doesn't remember. Your mother seems to have slipped partially back in time. How far back, I'm not sure, but it's far enough not to recognize some of the nurses and far enough to think your father is still alive. I was in with her for about ten minutes shortly after she'd come to, and in that time she asked twice when I thought Doyal would be in to visit her."

Remembering that Doyal was Elizabeth's husband, Jenny studied Rick's bewildered expression for several seconds. "How long has your father been dead?"

"Nearly six years," Rick answered, looking all the more perplexed.

"He died within four hours of having had a massive heart attack shortly after supper one night," Dr. Weathers explained. "We got him to the hospital within minutes and did everything we possibly could to keep him alive, but nothing worked."

"And she doesn't remember any of that?"

"Evidently not. Which is why I thought I'd better come by here and talk with you both about it." He then turned to face Jenny directly. "I especially wanted to talk to you. I know how very much you were looking forward to meeting your mother and I know how much she would have wanted to meet you, too, but I think we'd better put that on hold, at least until she's finally over this partial memory loss. I think introducing you to her right now would be too much strain."

"Of course, I understand," Jenny assured him. Though it broke her heart to have to put off the meeting indefinitely, she would not do anything that might in any way risk her birth mother's health. When she glanced over to see what Rick thought of this new development and glimpsed the compassion glimmering in his blue eyes, she suddenly had to blink back a fine sheen of tears.

Quickly she returned her attention to the doctor, who had reached forward to take her hand.

"I'm glad you are so understanding, because when Liz does get her memory back she'll be in for a very serious emotional blow. It will be like having Doyal die all over again. That's why I think it's best for us all to take a wait-and-see stance for the moment, at least until we know exactly how serious her amnesia is and how long it will take her to recover from it."

"But is it okay for me to visit?" Rick wanted to know.

"Not only is it okay, I recommend it. Someone needs to visit her regularly, so she won't dwell as much on the fact that Doyal isn't coming around like she thinks he should."

"What about Rachel?" Jenny asked. "If Elizabeth has slipped back in time, won't she expect Rachel to be a little girl?"

"She might. But I'm not trying to hide the fact she has amnesia from her," Dr. Weathers explained. "In fact, she's already vaguely aware something is wrong with her thinking. I think that's why she asks so many questions. Even so, it would be best to let her gradually come to terms with some of the things she seems to have forgotten."

"So it won't complicate matters any to take Rachel with me when I go at seven?"

"No. I think it will be perfectly okay to let Rachel go in. Fact is, seeing her might be just the catalyst Liz needs to start clearing up some of her present confusion," he explained.

"Then Rachel and I will both come. I'll pick her up after ball practice myself to make sure we make the seven o'clock visitation," he said, remembering how unreliable Rachel had been lately.

"And I'll stay away from the hospital altogether until you tell me it is okay for me to go," Jenny offered, eager to cooperate and far too relieved to learn their mother was off the critical list to feel much self-pity at the moment.

"Just don't you go running off back to West Texas," the doctor cautioned, then smiled encouragingly. "We still have my hide to consider."

"I'm not going anywhere," Jenny assured him, then returned his warm smile. "Your hide is safe with me."

Chapter Seven

Sick at heart over the prospect of having to put off meeting her birth mother indefinitely, Jenny stayed at Rick's while he and Rachel went on to the hospital shortly before seven o'clock. Although Jacqueline seemed to have accepted the fact that Jenny was to be treated as a welcome houseguest and did what she could to make her feel at home, Jenny was in too emotional a state to do much more than pace the floor of her bedroom.

When she heard Rick and Rachel return just minutes before eight, she hurried downstairs to find out how the visit had gone, eager to know if their mother had improved.

"She was in very good spirits and she recognized both of us immediately," Rick told her as soon as he had closed the back door and turned to face her. "But Dr. Weathers was right. She does have it in her head that Dad is alive. She asked me to stop by the warehouse on my way home and tell him that if he knows what's good for him, he'll stop working long enough to come by the hospital and visit her. She claimed that no matter how serious matters were at the warehouse, he could break away long enough to come by and see how she's doing."

"And what did you say to that?" Jenny asked, aware how difficult the situation must have been.

Although Jenny had directed the question to Rick, Rachel was the one who answered. "Actually, he was pretty cool about it."

Jenny glanced at her, surprised. That had been the first kind thing she had heard Rachel say about her father. Even during their indoor picnic earlier that afternoon, Rachel had seemed to be thoroughly enjoying herself but had managed to remain noticeably aloof when it came to her father. At times it had felt as if she were barely tolerating his presence, yet at other times she had laughed willingly at some of his antics, as if she had temporarily forgotten he was supposed to be the enemy.

"He told Grandma he would indeed stop by the warehouse before coming home because he had some papers he needed to pick up anyway, but warned her that there were a lot of pretty serious problems she didn't know about that were keeping Grandpa from being able to come visit."

"And she seemed to accept that," Rick added, sounding relieved that he hadn't had to be more deceptive. "She said that if that was true, if there were a lot of problems he didn't want to bother her with, then she'd try to be a little more understanding. But she did want me to do what I could to persuade him to go home long enough to get some rest. She's worried about his health." Tears glimmered in his eyes, forcing him to blink to clear his vision. "She also wanted me to make sure he's eating right. Dad was notorious for filling up on junk food whenever he was on one of his working binges.''

"I also told Grandma you were here waiting for permission to come see her," Rachel put in.

Jenny's heart jumped and when she glanced at Rick and noticed the quick breath he let out, she realized he had had a hard time handling that one. She looked at him apologetically before asking Rachel, "And what did she say when you mentioned my name?"

"I don't want to hurt your feelings or anything like that, but she doesn't seem to remember you just yet," Rachel continued, having missed the odd exchange between the adults. "But I told her how nice you are and that you were staying here with us until the doctor said it was okay for you to go visit her."

"And she didn't ask a lot of questions?" She hoped Rachel had not developed any suspicions when she discovered her grandmother did not know her.

"Oh, she asked plenty of questions," Rachel said. Her eyes rounded for emphasis. "But not just about you. About everything. She doesn't even remember what time of year it is. She wanted to know why I had on my baseball cap." Then Rachel's lively chatter turned suddenly solemn. "She also wanted to know where Mom was."

She cast an accusing gaze at her father. "I told her Mom wasn't feeling very good either and hadn't in months. I didn't mention the fact that she probably didn't even know Grandma was in the hospital."

"She knows" is all Rick would say on the matter. "But right now I think we've talked enough. You need to get upstairs and find your way into the bathtub and I have telephone calls to make."

For once, Rachel did not argue. Instead, she turned and headed immediately toward the nearest stairs, which were down the hall, just off the kitchen.

Rick waited until Jenny had completely disappeared from sight before returning the conversation to his mother. "She really did look a lot better. Her color is back and she was sitting up in bed reading one of her magazines when we first got there."

He indicated they should carry their conversation to the den with a quick, forward gesture of his head.

Jenny immediately started down the hall. "But she's still very confused?"

"Yes, she is," he admitted as he fell into step beside her. His gaze turned temporarily distant while he thought back on their short visit. "I guess I should have had the forethought to ask Rachel not to mention you just yet, but it never occurred to me she would think to bring up your name. She's usually very quiet whenever she visits anyone in the hospital. I think hospitals intimidate her, or at least they have ever since her grandfather died in one."

"Was Rachel there?"

By that time, they had arrived in the den. Jenny headed straight for the sofa and sat in the very same spot she'd taken when Dr. Weathers had come by earlier that day. Rick sat down beside her, only a few inches away.

"Yes, she was there. Rachel was staying at Mother's the night Dad suddenly collapsed. But because Mother could not locate Carla to have her come get her, Rachel ended up having to go with Mother to the hospital to wait out those four hours Dad was in Emergency. Rachel was only seven, so Mother didn't dare leave her at the house alone. Rachel was still there when Dr. Weathers came out to announce that it was over, that Dad just didn't make it."

"I can see why hospitals might intimidate her," Jenny said, wishing the girl had not been forced to go through something so traumatic, especially at such an impressionably young age.

"Tonight was the first night she really seemed to open up toward Mother since she was first admitted into the hospital. I guess, seeing how much better she looked, and having been told that she was suddenly recovering quickly, Rachel overcame some of her initial misgivings. But then again, part of the reason she was a little more willing to talk could have had something to do with the cheerful mood you put her in this afternoon. I want to thank you for that." He reached out and squeezed her hand in a show of how truly grateful he felt.

Jenny felt his warmth spread through her quickly. It was a warmth so profound, it lingered inside long after he'd taken his hand away and replaced it in his lap. "Thank me? For what? For helping her clean up the mess she'd made and sharing a few silly jokes with her?"

"For making her laugh. You don't know how long it has been since I've heard her laughter."

"Why is that?" Jenny asked, ready to know more about the strong resentment Rachel displayed toward her father. She felt she could be more successful in reaching Rachel if she better understood the problem that had arisen between the girl and her father. "Why does she become so upset whenever you are around?"

"I'm not sure, but I think she blames me for the divorce," he answered quite frankly.

"Why should she do that?"

"Because I was the one forced to tell her we were splitting up. Carla didn't stick around long enough to bother with telling Rachel goodbye. Rachel didn't even get a farewell note."

"Then the divorce was pretty much your ex-wife's idea?" she asked, wondering if that meant Rick still hurt from having been forced into something he did not want.

"It was *all* her idea. I happen to be the type who firmly believes in that trite little expression, 'for better or worse.' But Carla obviously had her own beliefs—none of which was in our wedding vows. Seems she had become bored with being a wife and a mother. She wanted to do something more exciting with her life than go shopping with her friends and take care of Rachel all day. She wanted the freedom to do what she wanted, when she wanted."

That sounded all too familiar to Jenny because Robert, too, had claimed he wanted more from life than simply being married to her. He had also suddenly decided he wanted the freedom to do what he pleased with whomever he pleased.

"So she asked for a divorce," she concluded, still wondering how that had affected him. Thus far he had not revealed what he actually thought about the matter. His expression was one of calm reserve.

"She didn't *ask*. She *demanded*," he corrected her, keeping his voice amazingly tranquil. "Although I knew she wasn't too thrilled with motherhood, because I had to practically bribe her to have Rachel, I still had no idea she was as unhappy as she eventually claimed to be.''

Rick was not certain why he had suddenly become so willing to tell Jenny about his divorce, but for some reason he wanted her to know. ''One Saturday afternoon a little over a year and a half ago, just a couple of weeks before Christmas, I came home early, wanting to spend the evening alone with her. Rachel had plans to spend that weekend at Mother's, so I knew we'd have the house to ourselves. I didn't tell Carla of my plans because I wanted to surprise her. Instead, I was the one in for a surprise.''

Jenny prepared herself for the worst, thinking he was about to tell her how he'd entered the house and found his wife in bed with another man. That was the one thing that could never be truly forgiven, the one pain that could never be completely forgotten. She knew, because although she could not be certain Robert had slept with Connie before he announced his desire for a divorce, it was clear he preferred his new-found friend over her.

''When I entered the house, I found a Dear John letter waiting for me on the kitchen table,'' Rick proceeded to explain. ''I then went upstairs to see if what the letter had said was true, if she had *really* left me, and discovered her closet stripped clean, as were two-thirds of all the drawers in our bedroom. The next morning her lawyer delivered the divorce papers, and while I was still at work that next day, she came back here and cleared out everything else she thought she deserved—including my grandmother's silver.''

When he looked at Jenny then she was surprised his expression was not glowering with anger. Instead there was only a distant sort of remorse darkening his blue eyes.

"My mother had given the silver to Carla years earlier, never dreaming that one day it would leave the family, so Carla had every legal right to take it. A couple months later I tried to buy it back from her, but she'd already sold it."

"I guess you harbor some pretty bitter feelings," Jenny said, thinking he concealed his emotions amazingly well.

"She could have handled it a little differently," he admitted. "But what I resent most is the way she continues to ignore Rachel."

"She does?" Jenny asked, finding that hard to believe. Earlier, Rachel had spouted nothing but praise for her mother.

"Yes. Although Carla has the legal right to visit with Rachel twice a month and could also have her for six weeks during the summer, she doesn't bother to do much more than make an occasional telephone call. She is too involved with her new boyfriend and with her budding career as a spokeswoman for some cosmetic company out of Dallas, to spend any time with Rachel."

"Then Carla now lives in Dallas?" Jenny asked, thinking the two-hour drive would make the trip all the more inconvenient. But even so, the woman should want to find the time to be with her own daughter.

"No, she lives in Longview, which is barely a thirty-minute drive from here. And she comes to Tyler fairly often, but it's always in the capacity of her job. Never to see Rachel. To tell you the truth, I'm getting tired of making excuses for her."

"Should you be doing that?" Jenny asked, thinking that could only lead to more trouble.

"I can't bear the thought of breaking Rachel's heart," he said, his expression revealing how vulnerable he was when it came to his daughter. "Despite everything, Rachel loves her mother dearly."

"And what about you? What do you feel for Carla?" Jenny asked, though she knew it was really none of her business. Yet for some reason it was important for her to know if he still loved his former wife.

"What do I feel for Carla?" Rick asked, repeating the question as if he had not given that much thought lately. "Disgust mostly. I gave up loving her months ago. I've even managed to get over my hatred of her. All I have left whenever I think of my ex-wife is a dull feeling of disgust."

Jenny felt encouraged by that response. It seemed a good indication that the pain and humiliation she still encountered whenever she thought of the cruel way Robert had treated her during her own divorce might eventually lessen until it became little more than a mere feeling of disgust. It was then she realized her anger toward her ex-husband had already diminished considerably. And now that she'd met Rick and learned what others had gone through, were still going through, she realized how easy she'd had it.

"But that's enough about Carla," Rick said, wanting to get off such a serious topic. "Let's talk about you. Did you make that telephone call you said you wanted to make?"

"Yes. I called Carole right after you left and told her what all has happened."

"Oh, then your call was to a female friend and not a male friend?" he asked, glad to hear it.

Jenny could tell he was feeling her out, trying to find out if she was involved with anyone, but after having asked so many personal questions about his life she could not really complain. "Yes, Carole is definitely female and she's certainly a friend. I guess you could say she's my very best female friend. She's always been there for me when I needed her most."

"It's good to have a friend like that," Rick commented, his gaze becoming distant again. "Here lately I've been so wrapped up in what has been going on at work and with my problems here at home, I haven't had much time for my friends, I'm sorry to say."

"I'm sure they understand," Jenny said, hoping to lessen his concern. "It can't be easy for you right now, what with your mother in the hospital and your daughter having such a hard time adjusting to her parents' divorce. I'm certain they understand why you haven't had much time for them lately."

"And I think, too, most of them feel it's just as well I stay away. I think they are still a little uncomfortable seeing me without Carla. I guess that's because most of my friends are married and I no longer am. Nor do I have a steady companion in my life right now. It makes me the odd man out."

"I know the feeling," she said, nodding in agreement. "Right after my divorce from Robert, you wouldn't believe the sudden drop in dinner and party invitations."

"You'd think being divorced meant automatic exile," he commented, then laughed and reached for her hand, this time for no other reason than he wanted to touch her. "I guess they think that divorce might be some sort of contagious disease."

Jenny's eyes widened again at the exhilarating effect his touch had on her.

Rick, too, was surprised, yet pleased by the strong chemistry that continued to pass between them. He hadn't reacted that strongly to a woman in a long, long while.

Although he might have been content to sit there holding her hand for quite some time, he realized his having her hand made her extremely uncomfortable. After a few more seconds, he released it. "I guess we'd better get on up to bed. I'll have a long day ahead of me tomorrow, if I hope to catch up on all the work I missed today."

Jenny quickly nodded her agreement, wanting to put as much distance as possible between them until she could better assess this strange physical attraction she felt for him. After all, he was practically her brother!

"Yes, it has been a long, tiring day," she said and stood, preparing to leave. It had been a day that had not turned out quite as she'd hoped, because she had yet to meet her birth mother, but it had been a pleasant day just the same.

Rick also stood. But neither he nor Jenny actually turned to leave. Instead they faced each other awkwardly for a long moment, just inches apart, each very aware of the other.

Although Jenny didn't really think Rick would have actually kissed her, she did wonder what would have happened had Rachel's music not blared down at them at that exact moment.

WITH ELIZABETH'S BLOCKAGE shrinking more every day, and her physical health improving immensely, Dr. Weathers decided to move her from ICU into a private room on the third floor a week later. Although she continued to remain very confused about a lot of things that had to do with the past, and continued to mix past events with those that had happened recently, everyone seemed pleased with her progress, especially Rick.

Every day, he came home with a glowing report about how well his mother was doing. Although Elizabeth continued to mention her husband and hinted often that she wished he would break away long enough to come see her, she willingly accepted the fact that he would be there if he could.

"I don't know how much longer I can keep up the pretense," Rick stated, after a particularly trying visit. "Although she's trying very hard to be understanding, she is starting to feel a little hurt by the fact he hasn't put aside his problems at work long enough to come by the hospital and see her. And now that she's in a private room, she wonders why he doesn't at least call. I'm surprised she hasn't tried to call him at work, if for no other reason than to make sure he's eating right."

"Do you think she would do that?" Jenny's eyes widened when she thought what might happen if she did try to call.

"She might. That's why I've already warned the women who answer the phone to expect such a telephone call. I've tried to explain the situation to them as best I can and have asked that they not take it upon themselves to inform her of the truth. I've told them to either put her through to me or take a message.''

Having come to realize that the warehouse Rick always talked about was a family business he now managed alone, Jenny felt certain the women would cooperate. "Glad you thought of that."

"Well, it was either tell them or have the telephone removed from Mother's room, and that would have caused her to become suspicious of my motives. She then would have started asking a lot more questions. This way, she has the reassurance of a telephone and I don't have to worry about her using it to find out the truth about Dad."

Jenny smiled. "She's lucky to have a son like you." It had been a genuine compliment, because Rick was clearly concerned about his mother's welfare.

She glanced at the clock, her eyes widening at the hour. "But right now you'd better concentrate on being a good father. Hurry upstairs and change. We don't want to be late for Rachel's ball game. It's scheduled to start promptly at eight o'clock, and it's nearly that now."

"I guess you carried her on over to the field at seven," he commented, remembering that had been the plan.

"Not only her, but Shelly and Sheila, too," she confirmed.

"You had to carry those two chatterboxes?" Rick asked, looking at her with true sympathy.

"I felt like I should. It really was Rachel's turn to supply the transportation. Besides, it was no bother. After all, what else do I have to do?"

"That's not the point. Here lately those girls have been asking you to drive them everywhere. You'd think they no longer had legs," he muttered. "If you don't put your foot down and tell them to find some other means of getting where they want to go, they'll have you wearing the tires right off your car."

"Doesn't matter. Compared to what it is costing you to feed me and what I'm saving by not having to stay in a hotel, I think the possibility of having to buy a new set of tires would be rather minor in comparison. Besides I enjoy spending some time with Rachel and her friends. We get along just fine."

"That in itself amazes me," Rick said with a chuckle. "Don't most thirteen-year-old girls generally tend to distrust adults?"

"Some adults, maybe," she admitted, also grinning. "The secret is to make them forget you're an adult. It's a little complicated, but the trick is to make them think of you as just another friend."

"That's some trick," he muttered, his mouth flattening into a straight line. "I wish you'd let me in on how you accomplish that."

"Well, in your case, I'm not sure it's possible. You are not just another adult. You're a parent. That automatically makes you their very worst adversary. No parent is to be trusted."

"Therefore I have no chance of ever becoming Rachel's friend," he concluded, his frown deepening at the reality in what Jenny had just said.

"Oh, you still have a chance—you just have to try harder, is all," she assured him. "But you need to keep in mind that a very thin line lies between being a parent and being a friend, and that dividing line really needs to be observed—from both sides.''

"Now you're starting to sound like a philosopher.''

"No, now I'm starting to sound like a high-school counselor, which is exactly what I am,'' she said, laughing in an effort to lighten the mood. "And I'm going to start sounding like a nagging housewife in a few minutes if you don't hurry upstairs and change.''

"Yes, ma'am,'' Rick responded dutifully, then hurried off to do just that.

Later, at the game, while Rachel was playing her usual position on third base, Rick noticed how well she and Jenny had started to get along. Whenever Rachel caught the ball and managed to get an opposing team member out, she would look into the stands to find Jenny, eager to see if she was cheering. Which Jenny always was.

Jenny also cheered for the rest of the team, encouraging Shelly to choke up on the bat more and instructing Sheila to lean into the ball better.

"I gather you like watching softball,'' he finally commented, after she had come up off the seat for what had to be the twentieth time in her latest effort to protest what she perceived as another bad call by the home-plate umpire. He had never seen anyone more enthusiastic about watching a simple softball game than Jenny.

"Sure, I like watching softball, but I like playing it even more. I played every summer when I was still in school,'' she admitted, then wiggled her eyebrows and buffed her fingernails on her collar as if to brag. "And I was darned good at it, too.''

Rick didn't doubt that for a minute.

"Why'd you ever quit? Don't they have women's softball leagues where you come from?"

"Not enough adults were interested—" she started to explain, only to come up out of her seat again to cheer a particularly good maneuver on Rachel's part.

"Did you see that double play?" she asked, her face filled with excitement. "You should be very proud of your daughter for having reacted so quickly."

"I am," he said, also standing to cheer, reminding everyone in the stands that that remarkable third baseman was his daughter.

Although Rick had always enjoyed Rachel's ball games, tonight he was having a lot more fun than usual. He decided that was because Jenny's enthusiasm was contagious. His eyes were glimmering with excitement when he cupped his hands to his mouth and shouted, "Keep an eye on that runner, Rachel. She's thinking about stealing third. You can see it in her eyes."

Rachel looked at him with surprise, then turned to do exactly what he had advised. She narrowed her gaze and nodded, as if daring the girl now on second to give it a try. The girl did indeed give it a try, at her coach's insistence, and Rachel had her out before she ever reached third base. Again Jenny and Rick came out of their seats to cheer Rachel's accomplishments.

All too soon the ball game was over, and after a short meeting with her team Rachel stumbled out of the dugout, tired but victorious.

"Looks like we just about have that championship all sewn up," she said proudly when she neared where Rick and Jenny stood waiting for her. "All we have to do now is win Friday's ball game against the Dodgettes, and that trophy will be all ours come end of the season."

"We'll just have to make sure you're up to it," Jenny commented, taking Rachel's glove from her and tucking it up under her own arm. "I guess I'll have to hit you a few more Friday afternoon."

"Just don't hit them as hard as you were hitting ·them today," Rachel complained good-naturedly. She pushed her hat back on her blond head and grinned. "There's really no point in it. There's nobody on any of the other teams who can hit the ball that hard anyway."

Rick looked at Jenny questioningly. "You practice ball with them?"

"Someone has to," Rachel put in, glancing back at the dugout with a disgruntled frown. "Coach called off our last two practices because he had somewhere he had to go. And he just told us that our Wednesday and Thursday practices have been called off, too. I guess he thinks we're so far ahead of the others that we can afford to slack off some, but that's not what we want to do. We want to get even better. We want to go through this entire season undefeated."

Afraid Rick was about to complain again that the girls were taking advantage of her, Jenny quickly added, "It helps pass the time. And gives me the chance for a little exercise. It makes me feel good to stay in shape."

Rick glanced down at the two long, slender legs protruding, sleek and tanned, from beneath a pair of white cotton shorts and decided her staying in shape made him feel good, too. But he worried that Jenny was spending too much time with Rachel.

He was afraid his daughter might be using Jenny to fill the void her own mother had left in her life and he knew if that proved to be the case, then Rachel was headed for another deep, emotional fall because Jenny, too, would one day leave her high and dry. Just like her mother, Jenny would eventually have to return to Stockfield and Rachel would again feel abandoned. He knew Jenny would not hurt Rachel intentionally, but she had a job waiting for her back in West Texas, and she had friends there.

Aware of how painful the mere thought of Jenny leaving was to him, he could well imagine how devastating it would be to Rachel, who was so very vulnerable right now. He worried that if the two continued to be so close, Rachel might take Jenny's leaving as a personal affront. He then wondered if he should discourage the two from spending so much time together.

But even if that might be the best thing for Rachel, he really didn't know how he would ever manage to keep the two apart. They were already such close friends. And aware of all the progress Jenny had made with Rachel in the very short time she had been there, he was not absolutely sure he should try to separate them.

Rachel needed someone like Jenny, someone older who was willing to take such a personal interest in her.

If only Jenny wasn't destined to leave, he'd believe her to be a true godsend.

Chapter Eight

It had been two weeks since Jenny first appeared at Rick's door, and in that time she had managed to become a very real and intricate part of both his and Rachel's lives.

Although Rick tried to face their time together with the very real knowledge that it would eventually all come to an end, he still worried that Rachel did not truly comprehend the fact Jenny would not always be there for them. One day, probably very soon, Jenny would return to her life in West Texas, coming back to Tyler for only an occasional visit, if that.

When he came right out and cautioned Rachel against the strong attachment she seemed to have developed toward Jenny, she had obstinately refused to listen. But then Rachel usually refused to heed much of anything he had to say these days.

Aware he was getting nowhere by discussing the situation with Rachel, he decided the time had come to discuss it with Jenny.

Rather than chance Rachel overhearing the conversation and in turn accusing him of interfering with her life, he decided to invite Jenny out to dinner the following Saturday, aware Rachel already had plans for Shelly and Sheila to sleep over that night.

He planned to take Jenny someplace with good food and a relaxed atmosphere, to be sure she was in an agreeable mood before suggesting she cut back on some of the time she spent with Rachel. He decided the perfect place to set the mood right was Johnny Cace's Restaurant, with its New Orleans atmosphere.

Although his worries concerning Rachel had remained foremost on his mind throughout the evening, Rick waited until they were nearly finished eating before finally bringing up the sensitive issue of what to do about his daughter.

"Rachel certainly has taken to you," he commented, approaching the subject in a roundabout way. "She likes you a lot."

"And I like her," Jenny said, smiling when she thought about how readily the girl had accepted her. "She is really a very nice girl at heart. She's just having a hard time right now sorting through some of her deeper feelings. But that's part of being thirteen."

"Is that why on some days she acts like she almost likes me, but other days she treats me like I'm the lowest form of life on earth?"

"Actually, she thinks Jamie Wilcox is the lowest form of life on earth," she said, hoping that might make him feel better. "But that's because he makes fun of her freckles."

"But she only has a few tiny freckles across her nose," Rick pointed out, thinking it odd that anyone would even notice.

"That's true, but I'm afraid Jamie Wilcox has excellent vision. And he's also very cute, which makes it all the worse."

"Don't tell me she's starting to become interested in boys," he said, his eyes widening with alarm. He had hoped that wouldn't happen for years yet.

"Not starting," Jenny corrected. "It is my understanding that she's been interested in Jamie Wilcox for well over a year, but all Jamie Wilcox seems interested in at the moment are his baseball cards and his dog, Barky."

"She's confided all this in you?"

Jenny nodded. "She wanted to know if I thought wearing makeup might help. I told her she was too pretty to start hiding it behind a lot of goop and that freckles were actually a sign of strong character."

"What else do you talk about?" he wanted to know, finding this sudden insight into his daughter's private feelings very interesting.

"You name it, we talk about it," she said with a slight shrug, unaware as of yet that this conversation had a direct purpose.

Rick dampened his lower lip with the tip of his tongue, then asked, "Do you ever talk about me?"

"Sure, all the time," Jenny admitted, dipping part of her shrimp into the bright red sauce that sat at the edge of her plate.

"Any of it any good?"

When Jenny glanced up to see the serious expression pulling at Rick's face, she decided to be truthful. He really wanted to know what his daughter thought of him. "Some of it is good."

NO RISK, NO OBLIGATION TO BUY... NOW OR EVER!

CASINO JUBILEE
"Match'n Scratch" Game

Here's how to play:

1. Peel off label from front cover. Place it in space provided at right. With a coin, carefully scratch off the silver box. This makes you eligible to receive one or more free books, and possibly other gifts, depending upon what is revealed beneath the scratch-off area.

2. You'll receive brand-new Harlequin American Romance® novels. When you return this card, we'll rush you the books and gifts you qualify for ABSOLUTELY FREE!

3. If we don't hear from you, every month we'll send you 4 additional novels to read and enjoy. You can return them and owe nothing but if you decide to keep them, you'll pay only $2.96* per book, a saving of 33¢ each off the cover price. There is *no* extra charge for postage and handling. There are *no* hidden extras.

4. When you join the Harlequin Reader Service®, you'll get our subscribers-only newsletter, as well as additional free gifts from time to time just for being a subscriber!

5. You must be completely satisfied. You may cancel at any time simply by sending us a note or a shipping statement marked "cancel" or returning any shipment to us at our cost.

YOURS FREE!

This lovely Victorian pewter-finish miniature is perfect for displaying a treasured photograph and it's yours absolutely free — when you accept our no-risk offer!

© 1991 HARLEQUIN ENTERPRISES LIMITED.

*Terms and prices subject to change without notice. Sales tax applicable in NY.

CASINO JUBILEE
"Match'n Scratch" Game

CHECK CLAIM CHART BELOW FOR YOUR FREE GIFTS!

YES! I have placed my label from the front cover in the space provided above and scratched off the silver box. Please send me all the gifts for which I qualify. I understand I am under no obligation to purchase any books, as explained on the opposite page.

(U-H-AR-10/91) 154 CIH ADE3

Name

Address   Apt.

City   State   Zip

CASINO JUBILEE CLAIM CHART

🍒🍒🍒	WORTH 4 FREE BOOKS, FREE VICTORIAN PICTURE FRAME PLUS MYSTERY BONUS GIFT
🍒🔔🍒	WORTH 3 FREE BOOKS PLUS MYSTERY GIFT
🔔🔔🍒	WORTH 2 FREE BOOKS

CLAIM N° 1528

HARLEQUIN "NO RISK" GUARANTEE

- You're not required to buy a single book — ever!
- You must be completely satisfied or you may cancel at any time simply by sending us a note or a shipping statement marked "cancel" or by returning any shipment to us at our cost. Either way, you will receive no more books; you'll have no obligation to buy.
- The free book(s) and gift(s) you claimed on the "Casino Jubilee" offer remains yours to keep no matter what you decide.

If offer card is missing, please write to: **Harlequin Reader Service**   P.O. Box 1867, Buffalo, N.Y. 14269-1867

"But not all of it," he stated, aware of what Jenny was being so careful not to say. "She's still angry with me about the divorce, isn't she? That's why she's always in such a hurry to push me away whenever I try to get too close, isn't it? She resents me for having allowed it to happen."

Jenny set her fork aside so she could give Rick her full attention, their conversation far more important than the shrimp left on her plate. "As you well know, Rachel has suffered a lot of chaos in her life recently. And it's not just the divorce that's causing her so much inner strife. It's a lot of things."

"Like what?"

"She worries about her grandmother, for one thing—and she also worries about her mother. She can't understand why her mother stays away. I think because she simply isn't prepared to cope with the fact her mother doesn't want her to be a part of her life right now, she has decided to blame you for Carla's constant absence. She hasn't actually come out and stated as much, but she clearly is not coping with the situation as well as she lets on, and it is her inability to cope that has revealed itself in the form of intense anger and resentment—both of which have unfortunately been directed toward you."

"But I have nothing to do with the fact her mother never comes to see her," Rick said, eager to defend himself.

"But Rachel doesn't know that, or perhaps it would be more appropriate to say Rachel doesn't *want* to know that."

Jenny reached forward and took Rick's hands in an effort to reassure him somehow, only to be reminded of how strongly the simple act of touching him affected her. Her pulse rate quickened as a result, but she did not pull away.

"Rick, try to understand. It will be a long time before Rachel gets over everything that has happened to her in the past couple of years. We really should try to go easy with her right now. She needs lots of space so she can try to sort through her feelings, yet not so much space that she feels neglected by you, too. It'll be a hard balance to find, but I do think we need to try to find it."

A strong current passed through Rick when he noticed how easily she had used the term "we." Clearly she wanted to be a part of Rachel's solution. But in doing so, would she unintentionally become a part of a larger problem? How much a part of their lives did she plan to become? And how much of their lives would she take with her when she left?

There was so much about Jenny he still did not know.

"Do you mind if I ask you a personal question?" he asked, pulling his hands away from hers so he could concentrate better on their conversation. Having her touch him proved to be too great a distraction. To give a reason for his abrupt action, he reached for his water glass.

"Depends on how personal," she responded, glancing at him with a raised brow, hoping they were about to get away from the delicate subject of Rachel, at least for a while. She was in too good a mood to talk about something so serious. "Just keep in mind, I refuse to give out my shoe size to anyone."

Rick chuckled at such an unexpected remark. "That's not what I was about to ask. What I want to know is why you waited until recently to start searching for your biological mother? You've known you were adopted all your life, haven't you?"

"Yes, I knew I was adopted, and I have always been curious about my ancestry, but not enough to launch an actual search. I guess the divorce really had a lot to do with it."

"How would your divorce affect such a decision?"

"I suppose, after having discovered how eager Robert was to cast me aside after ten years of what I presumed to be a very good marriage, I suddenly felt this strong personal need to know if my birth mother had felt that strongly about getting rid of me, too. I had to know if there was something about me that made people want to reject me. I realize it probably sounds a little strange, but I suddenly had an overwhelming desire to know the real reason I was put up for adoption. I still do. I want to know if I was given away because I simply was not wanted, or if it was because I could not be properly cared for otherwise."

"And you never wanted to search for your biological parents before the divorce?"

"Oh, I've always been curious about my biological parents and why they chose not to keep me, but out of respect for my adoptive parents I never bothered to find out anything about that part of my past. I didn't want them to feel threatened by my desire to know more about myself."

"And where are your parents now?"

"They died in an accident two years ago," she said, her eyes darkening with remembered pain. "Therefore, last winter, when I finally did decide to do something about finding my biological parents, I no longer had that protective need stopping me."

"How long did it actually take you?"

"Before I found out who my birth mother was and where I might find her? About five and a half months. Although I'd been tossing the idea back and forth in the back of my mind for several months before that, I didn't make the actual decision to finally do anything until my last birthday, which was in December."

"And were you terribly hurt when you thought you were finally going to get the chance to talk with your biological mother, after all that time, only to end up with me on the other end refusing to cooperate because I had decided you were just some saleswoman trying to meddle in my mother's life?"

"I think I was more angry than hurt," she admitted. "After all I'd gone through, after all the wild tales I'd had to tell and all the important people I'd had to face, I found myself unable to get past my own half brother."

"But I'm not really your half brother," he quickly corrected, wanting that point perfectly clear. "Because I was adopted, we are in truth no kin at all."

"I had no way of knowing that. All I knew at the time was that some man who had claimed to be my biological mother's son had stubbornly refused to tell me anything other than she was in the hospital. That's why I decided to come out here myself. I had to find some way to get around you."

"Which you promptly did," he remarked, remembering how easily she had convinced Dr. Weathers to cooperate, but only after having connived him into agreeing to go along with whatever the doctor decided. She was obviously not opposed to doing whatever was necessary to achieve what she wanted. He admired that about her.

Jenny chuckled when she noticed his raised eyebrows. "Well, after having confronted the hard-nosed department heads that work for the Department of Human Services in Austin, then a very serious-looking district judge in Denton County, and even having gone so far as to purposely misrepresent myself to a Nazarene preacher, I had a feeling I might be able to find some way around a bullheaded son like you."

"You had to go through all that just to get Mother's telephone number?"

"I had to do all that just to get her name and where she might be living now. From there, I had to con a telephone-company employee into getting Elizabeth Anderson's unpublished telephone number."

"Which she had to get shortly after Dad died because of the cruel prank calls she was getting," Rick said, nodding while he thought about all Jenny had gone through. "Mind-boggling," he commented, doubting he would have had the tenacity to have seen such an elaborate scheme through. "And here it is, nearly three weeks since your arrival and you haven't been allowed to meet her yet." He suddenly felt guilty, knowing she had been forced to wait so long. He wouldn't feel so badly if she weren't so darned understanding about the situation.

"Oh, but it's just a matter of time now," she said, hoping that would prove true. It had occurred to her in all that time that her biological mother might never overcome her struggle against amnesia, but she tried not to dwell on such a depressing thought. "Now that I have your full support, as well as the doctor's, all I have to do is wait for her to get better."

"To be perfectly honest, you don't have my *full* support in this matter," Rick told her honestly. "I still have some very grave doubts about all this, mainly because Mother never felt comfortable enough with that part of her past to confide in me. It must trouble her deeply."

Jenny's eyes widened with concern. Was he about to change his mind? Was Rick about to force her to go against him on this?

"But don't get me wrong," he continued, having seen the hurt and confusion filling her face. "I don't intend to do anything that can in any way prevent you from meeting her but I also don't plan to do anything that might *encourage* it, either. I'm sorry, but I still worry about how Mother will react to your sudden reappearance in her life."

"I appreciate your honesty," Jenny said, smiling faintly despite how uncomfortable she felt to discover he still had such doubts. "And I understand why you feel so concerned. I am also concerned. I worry constantly that I might be doing the wrong thing. Or that I might have already done the wrong thing by telling you. But whether right or wrong, meeting your mother is still something I intend to do. I've come too far not to give us at least one chance to get to know one another."

"But what if she doesn't get better soon? What if she can't shake her amnesia? Are you planning to stay on indefinitely?" He leaned forward, eager to hear her answer.

Jenny looked down at her napkin still in her lap and played absently with the corner while she thought about what she would do if Elizabeth Anderson did not get better soon. It was something she had not wanted to consider, but she knew it was a possibility.

When she finally realized the answers to his questions, she returned her gaze to meet his. "I'll try to stay as long as it takes. Or rather as long as I believe there is still a chance I will be allowed to meet her. As I told Dr. Weathers, I am scheduled to report to work the second week of July, which is still three weeks away. But if it turns out I have to stay a few days over that, then I will. I don't think I'll be fired for being a few days late."

That answer did not satisfy Rick. It was not what he had wanted to hear. "But what if after you do finally meet Mother, she tried to convince you to stick around for a while longer, so she can get to know you better? What if she wants you to stay here for the rest of the summer? What would you do about your job then?"

"I'm not sure," she said, not having given that much thought. "If it looked like I would be here that long, I would probably give Howard a call a few days before it was time for me to report in and let him know what had happened. He could then either find a temporary replacement to help with all the last-minute schedule changes, or he could have the school board fire me on the spot and hire someone else." Although she hoped it did not come to that, she knew it was a possibility.

"And who is Howard?"

"The principal at the high school where I work, who happens to have the entire administration wrapped around his finger. He's rather unpredictable at times, but I think he'd probably keep me on, out of sheer desperation. Unless, of course, he already has someone else in mind." For all she knew, he might have résumés from several other counselors sitting in a drawer somewhere waiting for the chance to see daylight.

Rick studied her for a few seconds. "You don't seem too concerned over the thought of losing your job."

"Although I don't think it would ever come to that, if it did happen I know I can always find another job at another school. There's always an opening somewhere for a high-school counselor. It happens to be one of those jobs with a high rate of burnout. In fact, I've threatened to quit on several occasions."

Rick chuckled. "Somehow I can't imagine you quitting at anything."

Jenny was surprised at the admiration she heard in his voice. It excited her to know he thought that much of her. "Why, thank you."

"And I can't imagine this Howard fellow ever deciding to fire you. That's why I wish you would taper off spending so much time with Rachel."

Jenny wrinkled her forehead. "I'm not sure I'm following this conversation. What does not losing my job have to do with Rachel?"

"Eventually you will be leaving us to return to that high school in West Texas," he stated quite frankly. "Therefore, I question this emotional risk you are taking with my daughter by having allowed yourself to become such close friends with her, when you know as well as I do you will eventually leave here and return home. Doesn't it bother you that Rachel is going to be terribly hurt by your leaving?''

"Not nearly as much as it bothered me to see such an unhappy child with no one to talk to."

"She has friends."

"I meant no one *older*. No one who knows enough to allow her simply to sort through all these mixed-up emotions she has jumbled up inside of her."

"She has me."

Thinking he was being extremely insensitive to Rachel's needs, Jenny felt her anger slowly rise, and with it so did her voice. "Why should she open up to you? She doesn't even trust you right now."

"Is that my fault?" Rick asked, his temper also flaring. His hands curled into hard fists where he rested them on the table beside his plate.

"I'm not sure whose fault it is. But it is definitely a fact. She doesn't trust you, and it may be quite some time before she ever learns to trust you again."

"You sound as if you agree with her," he accused, a muscle working angrily in his jaw. "You sound as if you think she just may be right about me."

"It doesn't matter if I agree with her or not. What matters is that she have someone to discuss it with. Someone who won't inject any personal opinions or try to lecture her about what she should or shouldn't do. Someone who will let her reach her own conclusions."

"And you have taken it upon yourself to be that someone," he commented, leaning back and crossing his arms, his hands still balled into fists. He was not quite sure why he felt so angry toward her when, in truth, he should be grateful for all she had accomplished in so short a time. But anger was exactly what he felt. Maybe it was because he didn't want her to leave anymore than Rachel would.

"I know I should have discussed it with you first, but yes I did take it upon myself to be that person. And to tell you the truth, I think I have already started to make progress with her. Far more progress than you could have ever made."

"Oh? Am I that inept as a father?" he asked, then turned in his chair to signal the waiter that he was ready for the check.

"It has nothing to do with your abilities as a father. It has to do with how she perceives you at the moment," she tried to explain, wondering how the conversation had ever become so hostile. She paused with what else she had to say when she noticed the waiter approach the table.

"Was everything satisfactory?" he asked, trying to pretend he hadn't noticed tempers were flaring at that table.

"Yes, everything was just fine," Rick muttered, jerking the check right out of the waiter's hands, then glancing at it. After seeing how much it was, he reached into his wallet and pulled out an ample amount of cash and tossed it onto the table. "Let's go."

Rather than continue their argument in front of the other patrons, Jenny waited until they were in the car before continuing. "I never meant to say you were a bad father and I don't see why you took it that way. All I said was that for some reason Rachel does not trust you right now."

"Well, if you've been having such deep, meaningful talks with her, then why don't you know what that reason is?" he asked as he reached down to put the car into reverse. The muscles in his jaw continued working rapidly back and forth.

"Because I'm letting her work out her emotions at her own pace, and she has yet to offer any reason why she feels the way she does," she answered, wondering why he sounded as if he was accusing her of something. "All I'm trying to do is be a sounding board for her. Can't you see that?"

"All I can see is that you've been interfering in my daughter's life ever since you got here," he muttered, quickly slamming the automatic shift into drive, then he turned determinedly silent when he pressed his foot against the accelerator.

Jenny sat in the passenger seat staring at the dimly lit street ahead, befuddled by his angry reaction, and angry with herself for letting it bother her as much as it did. After her divorce, she had resolved to stay as far away as possible from such determined, driven men—men who did not allow others to have opinions that varied from their own. Yet, there she was wishing she could find a way around Rick's anger so they could become friends again.

Still, she did not try to talk to him again until they had arrived back at the house.

"I don't understand why you are so angry with me," she finally found the courage to say, aware when he did not immediately get out of the car and rush around to her door, she would have to open it herself this time. After she'd stepped out of the car, she turned to close the door and watched while he finally climbed out of the car and came around to her side. "What have I done that was so terrible?" she asked, when he stopped just a few yards away.

"What have you done?" he asked, as if unable to believe she didn't know. He waved his hands to emphasize how strongly he felt about what he had to say. "First, you come waltzing into our lives out of nowhere, then proceeded to politely charm the socks right off of us, making us extremely fond of you, when all the while you knew you would be leaving us."

"Us?" Jenny asked, aware he had included himself. "I don't understand. I thought we were talking about Rachel."

He took several more determined strides toward her until he stood directly in front of her, blocking her path to the outside. The only light that spilled into the darkened garage came from the iridescent glow of the security light outside.

"I was talking about Rachel. But I'm talking about me, too. About us." He reached out to take her shoulders in a surprisingly tender grasp and pulled her toward him. "Can't you see how terribly fond I've become of you? How very much I desire you?"

"But you're my brother," she reminded him, searching his expression through the shadows that surrounded them, aware of how incredibly good his hands felt on her shoulders, despite the fact he was babbling such nonsense.

"Will you quit saying that?" he said, his voice low and determined. "I am no more your brother than—than—" he frantically sought a name "—than Dr. Weathers is my sister. Why can't you see that?"

"B-but we have the same mother," she quickly pointed out, feeling more and more uncomfortable with the strong physical arousal she felt whenever she was near him. How she longed to know what his kiss was like. Even though she knew it was wrong to want to experience such a thing, she could not deny the overwhelming attraction she felt for him and had from the very first day they had met. If only the situation were different. If only she felt free to explore these passionate feelings.

"Technically, and by birthright, Elizabeth Anderson is your mother and not mine," he said, trying to find just the right words to explain the circumstances the way he perceived them. "But legally, she's *my* mother and not yours."

"Therefore we both share the same mother," she concluded with a puzzled expression. She thought it odd that he would argue against himself like that.

Rick let out an exasperated breath. "But that still does not make us brother and sister."

"What does that make us?" she asked, tilting her head so she could better see his face in the pale blue light that trickled in from outside.

Rick thought about that a long moment before finally answering, "Confused as hell."

Jenny couldn't help but laugh. "You have finally said something I can thoroughly agree with."

"Then why can't you agree that we are not really brother and sister? Just because my mother happens also to be your mother does not make us blood-related." He paused while he considered what he'd just said. Slowly a grin stretched across his face causing two long, narrow dimples to form in his cheeks. "Mind-boggling, isn't it?"

"It definitely boggles my mind," she agreed, also grinning, pleased to hear the anger gone from his voice.

Rick studied the sparkle in her eyes for a moment, then turned his gaze to her slightly parted lips, still curved into a partial smile. "And don't go trying to turn the fact that we both have such easily boggled minds into further evidence that we just might be true brother and sister. That's about the only thing we do happen to have in common—traitwise, that is."

"Oh? And what else might we have in common?" Jenny asked, her heart racing, aware he had slowly begun to lean forward, his gaze focused on her mouth as if drawn toward it. She blinked hard when she tried to decide what she should do about this new predicament, if anything.

Her common sense told her she should pull away and try to distract him with silly chatter, but her heart refused to obey. She simply did not possess the strength she needed to actually do what she knew was right—nor did she have the desire.

Instead of pulling away, she stood perfectly still, staring at him through the darkness, mesmerized by their closeness. Every nerve ending in her body was alive and tingling with anticipation and she discovered she could hardly breathe when he then paused. His parted mouth was just inches from hers when he brought his tender gaze up to touch hers again, as if in some way testing her.

Able to see the desire glimmering from the very depths of his blue eyes, Jenny felt whatever resistance she might have clung to slowly slip away, vanishing into the darkness.

The deep, undeniable yearning she felt for him defied all reason. It had consumed her like a slow fever. Searing right into her very soul. Leaving her feeling weak yet surprisingly strong.

It was then she knew she would let him kiss her. More than anything on this earth, she wanted Rick Anderson to kiss her. She wanted to know what it was like to be held passionately in his arms, his mouth pressed hungrily against hers—if only for a moment.

"We have *this* in common," he murmured, then gently lowered his lips to hers.

Jenny was unprepared for the sheer power behind Rick's kiss, unprepared for how quickly her senses were sent reeling inside her. She was not sure how to handle such a surprisingly potent reaction. Part of her still thought she should do the right thing and pull away, because there was a family link between them, however slight. But another part of her, a stronger, more brazen part of her yearned to explore these exhilarating feelings further.

It had been years since she'd been held in a man's arms with such passion, years since she had felt such an overwhelming desire to respond to that passion. Every fiber of her being ached with her sudden need.

Weakly she leaned against him, tiptoeing forward in her eagerness to press every inch of her body against every inch of his. Although that tiny part of her still nagged that her reaction was wrong, her body had decided that kissing him in such a passionate way felt right.

Closing her eyes she pressed closer still, accepting the kiss he offered with the hunger of a woman who had denied her own needs for far too long. Eagerly she yielded to his kiss and when his arms slipped possessively around her, surrounding her with an intoxicating warmth, her thoughts went beyond the kiss and into the wonder of what it must be like to have someone like Rick make love to her—someone so determined and strong, yet so surprisingly gentle.

The kiss deepened and Rick pressed her harder against him, flattening her breasts, stomach and thighs intimately against his strong, muscular body.

A burning heat settled deep at the very core of Jenny's being, and at that moment she knew she wanted him more than she had ever wanted any man—even though a part of her still felt it was wrong to feel that strongly about her birth mother's son, adopted or not.

While still holding Jenny close, Rick's embrace loosened and he moved his hands first to caress the small curve of her back, then downward to press against the gentle roundness of her hips, and finally to stroke the sensitive area along her rib cage. Even through the thin materials of her dress and undergarments, his touch seared her skin. A liquid fire coursed through her veins, sending a sensual heat to every fiber of her being—and when he brought one hand up to cup one of her aching breasts, caressing the rigid tip with his thumb right through her clothing, she moaned aloud at the resulting sensation.

She wondered if she dared let the kiss progress any further. It had been so long since she'd been made love to, *really* been made love to.

But was this truly the right time? And would it be for the right reasons? What would then happen when the time did come for her to return home? If she allowed herself to share such intimacy with Rick, she would run the very real risk of falling deeply in love with him and that would never do. It would make leaving too painful to bear.

It was then, while she worried about her own pain, that Jenny realized why Rick had seemed so concerned about her relationship with Rachel. By having allowed such a close, personal relationship to develop, she would have no choice but to hurt the child when the time came for her to leave. Why had that not occurred to her before she had allowed herself to become so involved? And why hadn't it occurred to her how very much it would in turn hurt her to leave Rachel and Rick behind.

Still, she'd made such progress with the child, just as she had made progress with the father.

If only life could be more simple.

If only she felt right about letting Rick make love to her.

But she didn't, and with trembling hands she finally found the strength she needed to push him away.

"It's getting late," she said in an emotionally strained voice. "I'm sure the girls are wondering what happened to us." Then without giving him the opportunity to do or say anything that might change her mind, she pushed past him and hurried toward the house, her heart pounding so hard against her breastbone she thought it would break through the ribs that surrounded it and fly right out of her chest.

Chapter Nine

"I know you said you had a lot of other things to do this afternoon, but could you take me over to Grandma's house first?" Rachel asked, her pretty face drawn into such a pensive expression that Jenny would have to have been made of stone to refuse. "I'd walk, but it's just so blasted hot outside."

Jenny glanced up from the mirror while she finished brushing her hair, nearly ready to leave. "Why do you need to go to your grandmother's?"

"Because this is Monday and I haven't watered her plants since last Tuesday," she said, twisting her forehead into a guilty frown. "It's my turn to water them and I was supposed to go over there Saturday to water them, but I forgot. And then Shelly and Sheila stayed too late for me to have time to take care of it yesterday."

Although Jenny had made the difficult decision to try to spend considerably less time with Rachel, she did not like the thought of the girl walking the seven blocks in ninety-eight degree heat, especially with such unbearable humidity. "Okay. I'll take you. But you'll have to hurry. I do have some shopping I want to do."

"Shopping? Is that what you're planning to do today? I love shopping," Rachel responded, her blue eyes sparkling with sudden enthusiasm. "And with Shelly at her grandmother's until Wednesday and Sheila having to take summer school for the next six weeks, I don't have anything else to do."

Jenny moaned inwardly, knowing she was about to go against her better judgment and invite the girl to go along with her. "I was planning to go to the mall and look for a new pair of running shoes. Although I don't really do a lot of running, I have somehow managed to wear my big toe right through my favorite pair."

"I know just the place," Rachel assured her. "The same place where I got my baseball cleats. They've got every kind of sport shoe imaginable. We'll go there first. Then we can stop by Grandma's on the way back."

"No, I think we'd better stop by Grandma's on the way over. If those plants haven't had water since last Tuesday, they are probably pretty thirsty by now." She frowned, wondering if Carole was being as lax about watering her own plants.

"Whatever," Rachel said agreeably. "When do you want to leave?"

"Now is as good a time as any," Jenny said, sighing softly as she set her brush aside. She knew it would be wise to be finished and back home before Rick returned for the day. Although he had not mentioned again how concerned he was with all the time she spent with Rachel—not since the argument they'd had Saturday night—she knew he still worried about it. And with good reason. "Go get your purse. I'll tell Jacqueline where we're going and will meet you in the car.''

Ten minutes later, they both were on their way.

Although Jenny tried not to show it, she was extremely excited over the prospect of seeing the inside of her birth mother's house. She did not want Rachel to think she was more curious than she should be about the woman's home, but she could hardly wait to see if the place was as grand on the inside as it had looked from the outside.

As soon as she had stopped the car on the section of drive Rachel had indicated was nearest the back door and realized that Rachel intended to go on in without her, she quickly volunteered her help.

When she followed her bouncy niece through a tall privacy fence, across a lovely bricked patio and into the house through a sliding-glass door, Jenny felt a strange, almost eerie sensation wash over her. She felt a sudden nearness to the woman who'd given birth to her. Being right there, in her birth mother's own house, surrounded by all her personal things, was almost like sharing a moment with the woman herself.

''I'll get the plants upstairs while you water the ones down here,'' Rachel said, hurrying to the other side of the skylighted kitchen to retrieve a couple of plastic water pitchers from a small cabinet near the kitchen sink. ''You'll discover that there are plants in almost every room in this house. A few of them are silk and don't need watering, but most of them do.''

She grinned when she glanced back over her shoulder at Jenny. ''Sometimes it's kinda hard to tell the real ones from the silk ones. Don't tell anyone how dumb I was, but I actually watered the big tree near the front door three times before I realized it was a fake.''

Quickly she snatched two half-gallon pitchers from the shelf and bent over the sink to fill them with water. When she did, she turned the pressure on too hard and sprayed her white jumpsuit with a high blast of water but did not seem too concerned, nor did she seem too surprised.

''Grandma sure loves her plants,'' she explained, instinctively reaching for a nearby dish towel to dab some of the water off her clothing as if spraying herself might be a common occurrence. ''After we get through in here, I'll have to go outside and water some of the flowers out front. She's got automatic sprinklers that water the lawn and get most of her flower beds, but they don't catch the flowerpots up on the porch. Won't take me long.''

Accepting one of the pitchers of water, Jenny turned and headed first to a thirsty violet growing on a nearby windowsill, then toward a drooping ficus near a window a little farther away, then on toward the nearest door. ''I'll meet you back here when I finish.''

''There are nine rooms downstairs and at least one real plant in every one, even in the bathroom. Be sure you get them all,'' Rachel cautioned before disappearing through another door.

With Rachel in another part of the house, Jenny felt free to explore her surroundings more closely. Having gone through a wide swinging door that entered into a large dining room, she stood in the center of the room and carefully studied how elegantly the room had been decorated. She wondered if her birth mother had personally picked out the scroll-footed dining ta-

ble or if she'd hired an interior decorator to select her
furnishings.

Whichever was the case, the room was tastefully
done.

After watering the two massive ivies and the huge
fern that grew near the multipaned dining-room windows and a tall, lumbering rubber plant that stood
guard beside the hallway door, Jenny gave the dining
room one last memorizing glimpse then proceeded
eagerly into the next room.

She was not too surprised to next enter an enormous living room with thick gray carpeting and white
paneled walls. A nine-piece rococo sofa set faced a
huge, elaborately crafted fireplace in a wide semi-
circle and a large piano stood off to one side, near a
wide set of windows.

Jenny's breath caught in her throat when she moved
closer and noticed a varied assortment of framed
photos scattered across the top of the piano. Swallowing to force the constriction down, she headed toward
the photographs, her whole body feeling suddenly
weak yet vibrantly alive.

Tears filled her eyes when she came near enough to
see the largest of the pictures, which was an outdoor
family grouping that featured Rachel and Rick and
two women Jenny did not immediately recognize, one
of which she believed would be her birth mother.

It was not until she stepped closer and blinked several times to clear her tear-blurred vision that she saw
her birth mother's smile for the first time. And what
a charming smile it was. The sort of smile that included even her eyes. A smile so wide and so all-

consuming, it formed two profound dimples, one in either cheek, and brightened the entire room.

A smile very much like her own, Jenny realized.

Gently, reverently, she set the water pitcher aside and picked up the framed photograph so she could look at it more closely, quickly memorizing every detail of her birth mother's face.

It was hard to imagine that this was the same woman she had seen in the hospital just a few weeks ago. There was so much life, so much vitality in her face—so much love for those around her.

Jenny then turned her attention to the other three people in the picture, people her birth mother obviously loved tremendously.

Rachel was seated on a small outdoor bench beside her grandmother, grinning as widely as her girlish cheeks would allow, clearly delighted to be having her picture taken. Her hair had been pulled into a long, bouncy ponytail high at the back of her head and she was dressed in a light pink sundress.

Jenny felt her heart take a funny little jump when she noticed Rick next. He was also smiling. He stood just behind his mother, dressed handsomely in white casual slacks and a pale blue pullover shirt, his left hand draped casually over his mother's shoulder. Jenny next noticed a woman who looked to be in her mid-twenties and stood just behind Rachel and off to the right of Rick. She wore a bright red flowing jumpsuit with a decorative white belt and a red-and-white wide-brimmed hat that made her look as if she had just stepped out of a fashion magazine.

Although Rachel and her grandmother were holding hands and Rick's hand rested lightly on his mother's shoulder, Jenny noticed the other woman in the photo touched no one. Nor was her beautiful smile quite as genuine.

If that was Carla, Jenny wondered how Rick had not noticed the woman was unhappy. Despite the smile she had plastered across her pretty face, she looked as if she would rather be anywhere else than with her own family having an outdoor photograph made. Jenny felt it sad that the beautiful young woman could not have enjoyed herself in the same way the others were enjoying themselves.

"You curious to see what my mom looks like?" Rachel asked, startling Jenny out of her quiet reverie.

Actually, no, I was more curious to see what my own mom looked like, thought Jenny, but she dared not say that aloud. "To tell you the truth, I was looking at all of you. This is a very lovely picture."

Rachel nodded that she agreed and came forward to tell her more about it.

"That picture was made two summers ago out in Grandma's backyard. She wanted a picture with that huge wall of honeysuckle in the background, so she had Uncle Shawn take this one. Uncle Shawn is Grandma's brother," Rachel explained. She reached forward to point to the tiny white and yellow flowers sprinkled across a wall of greenery behind them, her voice full of affection. "Grandma loves the smell of honeysuckle in the spring."

While Jenny absorbed the fact she had an uncle somewhere named Shawn, Rachel immediately reached for another photograph and showed it to her, eager for her to see them all.

"This one was taken when I was about five or six. We were all up in Oklahoma at a place called Turner Falls. That cabin in the background was where we stayed. That's my Grandpa holding up the big fish. He was always a lot of fun. They say I caught that fish, but I really don't remember."

Smiling fondly, Jenny studied the face of the man who had eventually married her birth mother. He looked tall, thin and happy. Kind of like her own father had been. For some reason that pleased Jenny immensely, pleased her to know her birth mother had been married to a man who looked like he truly knew how to enjoy life.

Rachel's face remained bright with enthusiasm when she snatched that photograph away from Jenny, then reached for yet another one, promptly putting it in front of her. "This one is of me and Mom when I was about three. I wasn't really a ballerina. I just had a ballerina outfit I liked to play in back then. That was before I found out baseball was more fun."

Jenny tried to see what Carla's expression might have been, but before she could really detect much, Rachel had taken that one from her, returned it to the piano and reached for yet another, pleased to have someone who seemed so interested in her grandmother's photographs.

"And this one was taken just a couple of months ago over at our house, out near the rose garden beside the garage. There's Uncle Shawn, so I guess Aunt Nicolle took this one." She watched while Jenny bent closer to study her uncle's face, then suddenly Rachel's expression changed into one of clear resentment when she then added, "Of course, Mom isn't in this one. Dad doesn't like for her to come around much anymore. Hasn't since the divorce.''

"It sounds as if you think your father is trying to keep you and your mother apart," Jenny said, keeping her gaze centered on the photo and not on Rachel. She wanted the girl to think she was only casually interested in whatever she had to say.

"That's because he is," she said with an obstinate toss of her head. "Why else would Mom stay away like she does? I don't know what it is that Dad holds over her, but he sure likes to use it. It's been nearly two months since I last saw my mom, and then it was only for an hour." Her lower lip trembled when she considered how unfair that was.

"But I don't understand. Why would your father want to keep you two apart?"

"I don't really know, unless maybe he's jealous of her. Or maybe he's afraid I'll want to go live with her, instead of stay here with him." Her nostrils flared when she then added, "He's *very* possessive."

"He is?" Jenny asked, thinking that was a strange thing to say. He had not seemed so very possessive to her.

"Yes. Every single time I leave that house he demands to know where I'm going, how I'm going to get there and who I'm going to be with. If he's not home to tell, then I have to tell Jacqueline." Her eyes narrowed resentfully. "I can't go anywhere without telling someone exactly where I'm going, who I'll be with and when I'll be back."

Jenny didn't think that was being possessive; she thought that was merely being concerned. If she was ever lucky enough to become a parent, she'd do the exact same thing. "What else does he do?"

Rachel thought about it, then shrugged. "That's about it, I guess. Other than being too possessive and trying to keep my mom and me apart, he can be a pretty okay dad. All my friends like him."

Jenny wondered exactly how much she should say. "But are you absolutely positive your father is the reason your mother stays away?"

"Has to be. Why else would she?"

"I don't know," Jenny answered carefully. "Maybe she's very busy right now, trying to get her new life in order."

"She's had over a year to get her new life in order. Besides, she'd still find time for me. She always did before," Rachel insisted, then lowered her eyelashes to reveal the depth of her suspicions. "Dad claims she's been sick a lot lately and that's why she never comes over. But that's just what he wants me to believe, and that's why he rarely ever lets me talk to her when she calls."

"And how can you be so sure that's what he wants you to believe. Maybe your mother really has been sick," Jenny suggested, then mentally added, *if not physically, then perhaps emotionally.*

"Because I know better. Sheila and Shelly saw Mom at the mall a few weeks ago and said she looked healthy enough to them. She was demonstrating cosmetic techniques in one of the fancier department stores and Shelly said she couldn't have looked healthier."

Jenny fell silent for a moment while she more fully absorbed everything Rachel had just told her. Obviously by having covered up the real reasons behind the woman's absence the way he had, Rick had unwittingly made himself out to be the villain. And knowing Rachel would probably think she was merely taking her father's side because they had managed to become such close friends in the three weeks she'd been there, Jenny decided not to bother explaining the situation as it had been explained to her. Rachel would only resent her, too, for having taken his side.

Instead of coming readily to Rick's defence, Jenny decided to take a whole different approach. She would encourage Rachel to discover the truth for herself.

"If you truly believe your father is trying to keep you two apart, then why don't you do something about it?"

"What can I do?"

"Call her. If you truly believe that your father is not being completely honest with you about your mother, quit allowing him to be the go-between. Call her and talk to her yourself. Tell her how you feel. See what you two can work out on your own."

Jenny knew the telephone call would produce one of two results. Either Rachel would find out for herself that her mother had lost all interest in anything having to do with her previous life, including her family—or Carla would come to her senses upon hearing her daughter's voice and realize Rachel needed her. Either way, Rachel would come out ahead. She might be hurt in the process, should her mother not come to her senses, but Rachel would finally know the truth. She just hoped Rick did not become too angry with her for having suggested such a thing.

She shuddered when she remembered just how angry he'd been Saturday night. Like Robert, Rick had a volatile temper, but unlike Robert, Rick's anger had developed out of a deep concern for someone else: his daughter. Whenever Robert had become that angry, his concern was usually for himself.

That was where the difference lay between the two men. Rick might act a lot like Robert at times, and even walk in that same cocky manner, but that was about as far as the similarities went. Robert was incapable of showing the tenderness Rick showed toward Rachel, nor had he ever kissed her with quite the same honest passion—or at least he hadn't during the last several years of their marriage. And Robert was incapable of forgiveness.

She just hoped that proved to be another difference between the two men. Her heart constricted at the thought Rick might never forgive her for the part she'd played in getting Rachel to telephone her mother. She cared too much for him to want him angry with her. But the fact was, her suggestion that Rachel call her mother and try to work things out was as much for his benefit as it was Rachel's.

Until Rachel finally learned the unfortunate truth about her mother, the situation between her and her father would only grow worse and that would not only prove detrimental to both their happiness—it was utterly senseless. She had to do something, even if it meant risking her own relationship with the two.

"But I don't even know her telephone number," Rachel complained, her dark blond eyebrows drawn low to reveal the hopelessness of the situation.

Already aware of all the tricks when it came to finding out telephone numbers, Jenny shrugged. "That shouldn't be any problem. If for some reason the number turns out to be unlisted, all you have to do is get your hands on a few of your father's telephone bills. I'm sure at one time or another he has called her, and if that's so, her number will be on his phone bill. But chances are, all you will have to do is call directory assistance to get the number. For some reason, I don't think your mother will have an unlisted number." But, then, she hadn't expected her birth mother to have an unlisted telephone number either.

"I'll do it," Rachel said, her blue eyes widening with determination. "I'll call Mom just as soon as I get home. And if she's not there when I first call, I'll keep right on calling until I finally get to talk to her." An excited smile lit her face. "Who knows? Maybe she'll come get me and let me spend a week or two with her. Or if she can't come get me, maybe you could take me over there. I'd pay for your gasoline."

"I'm not worried about the gasoline. But you'd better wait to see what she says before you start making a lot of plans," Jenny cautioned her, not wanting the girl's disappointment to be too great. Her stomach tightened into a painful knot at the thought of how deeply Rachel would suffer when the truth first came out, but she kept reminding herself it was for the best. "She may be too busy for visitors right now. After all, she has a job now and I'm sure that takes up a lot of her time."

But Rachel refused to let that concern her. "Surely she gets weekends off. I'll go stay with her over the weekend. I hear Longview had a really awesome mall.

We can go shopping together and then maybe go to the movies."

Thinking it was time to get off that subject and onto something else, before Rachel worked her hopes up any higher, Jenny reached for the water pitcher she had set aside and asked, "Well, if we are ever going to get back home so you can make your call, we'd better hurry with all the other things we have to do. Have you finished watering the plants upstairs?"

"Sure have," Rachel told her, indicating, with a slight nod, the empty pitcher she had held when she first came into the room. "All I have to do now is water the flowers out front and we'll be ready to go."

"While you do that, I'll finish with the ones downstairs."

"You're not through yet?" Rachel asked, her nose wrinkling at the thought of anyone being so slow.

"Not yet. But I should be through by the time you are," she stated, then hurried from the room to finish.

Alone again, Jenny wondered if she had done the right thing by encouraging Rachel to call her mother. If the girl ended up being terribly hurt and Rick then found out it was all her idea, he might truly never forgive her, and the thought of Rick hating her made her stomach ache. He'd been so kind to her over these past few weeks, so terribly solicitous—though not always in a brotherly fashion—and in response she had become far too fond of him to want him angry with her. Then, too, she'd also come to care too much for Rachel to want her deeply hurt by her own mother's rejection.

Still, she had to try to get Rachel and Rick back together. One way or another, Rachel needed to find out, and on her own, that her father had nothing to do with her mother's continued absence.

It was nearly five o'clock before Jenny and Rachel returned to the house, having spent longer shopping for shoes and various other items than they had first expected.

Because Rick had been coming home between five-thirty and six almost every afternoon since Jenny's arrival, Rachel hurried into the den to make her telephone call, wanting to get it done before he got there. Jenny followed to make certain she was able to get the telephone number she needed. But because the telephone number was indeed listed, all Rachel had to do to obtain the correct number was call directory assistance. By five-fifteen, Rachel had punched the numbers into the telephone and sat back to wait, her blue eyes wide with anticipation.

"I'll leave so you can have your talk in private," Jenny said, thinking she would want to be alone.

"No, stay," Rachel said, reaching to grasp her by the arm. She made no comment as to why she wanted her there, but Jenny could tell by Rachel's expression that it was important she not be alone, so she stayed.

After several seconds, Rachel's expression fell and she returned the receiver to the telephone base with a disappointed slam. "It's busy. Can you imagine? After all that, it's busy."

Jenny tried not to grin, remembering a similar incident that had happened just a few weeks ago. "Let's give her five minutes, then call again. Your dad shouldn't be home for fifteen or twenty minutes yet."

Rachel paced the floor while Jenny watched until finally five minutes passed.

"Try again," Jenny encouraged after having glanced at the clock. Her heart hammered wildly when she realized the line might still be busy, forcing them to wait even longer. Aware Rick could be home any minute now, she listened carefully for the familiar sound of his car pulling up into the drive.

Rachel did as she was told. Perching precariously on the arm of the sofa, facing the end table, she bent forward and pressed the numbers on the telephone. When she straightened, she looked at Jenny and took a deep breath.

"It's ringing," she said, her voice barely above a forced whisper.

Aware the moment had arrived, Jenny bit into her lower lip while waiting to see what would happen next.

Rachel's gaze drifted toward the ceiling, her expression starting to reveal further disappointment. "That's the fifth ring and no one has an—" Her eyes stretched wide for a second, then she looked somewhat perplexed. "Is this Carla Anderson's residence?"

She glanced at Jenny with a knitted brow when she then asked, "May I speak to her?"

While waiting for her mother to come on the line, Rachel put her hand over the mouthpiece and frowned. "Some man answered the phone, but he's gone to get Mom." She put the receiver back to her ear but kept her hand in place. "Sounds like she's having a party."

"Hello, Mom? This is Rachel," she said, her voice filled with emotion. She paused to swallow then responded, "At home—no, Dad isn't even here. No—yeah—no—sure, I'll be home except maybe for about thirty minutes right around seven. At the hospital visiting Grandma. When do you think they'll leave?—okay, sure—no, I'll be up—fine—okay, goodbye."

When she bent forward to return the receiver to its base, her expression was uncertain. "She has a lot of friends over right now and can't talk, but she's going to call me back as soon as they leave. She said it might be nearly eleven o'clock before she calls, but I told her that would be okay."

"But you're usually asleep by then," Jenny said, wondering what Rick would think when suddenly Carla decided to call Rachel and so late at night. He would no doubt want to know what was going on and Rachel would have to tell him. And when she did, she would also have to tell him it was all done at *her* suggestion.

Jenny just hoped he would understand her reasoning when she tried to explain it to him.

"I told Mom I'd still be awake," Rachel said. "Besides, I couldn't sleep anyway, knowing she's planning to call me back."

"Did she sound surprised to hear from you?"

"Sure did," Rachel said, then narrowed her blue eyes in an obvious display of bitterness. "She wanted to know if *Dad* knew I had called. I could tell by the tone of her voice that she felt pretty certain he would disapprove of my calling."

Jenny closed her eyes against the sudden pain that pulled at her chest because she, too, felt certain he would disapprove. Until now, he had gone to great lengths to protect Rachel from the painful truth. He would not take too kindly to someone purposely undermining his efforts to protect his own daughter.

That night during supper, Rick noticed something was bothering Rachel more than usual. He kept looking at her with a pensive expression until finally he asked, "Why aren't you eating?"

Rachel glanced at his plate and noticed it was nearly empty, then glanced guiltily at all the food left on her plate.

"It looks to me like I'm not very hungry," she snapped, then looked as if she immediately regretted having done so. She brought her troubled gaze up to meet Jenny's, as if to ask for her intervention.

Knowing Rachel had enough to worry about at the moment, Jenny quickly came to the rescue. "I imagine her lack of appetite had something to do with those chocolate-covered doughnuts we purchased this afternoon. I told her she should only have one, but she insisted she wanted two." Jenny did not mention that, in the end, Rachel had eaten neither. The poor girl had been too excited about what might happen when she did finally call her mother to do more than fidget with the sack in the car. By the time they had arrived home, the doughnuts were too mangled to eat.

"Where'd you get doughnuts?" Rick asked, turning his gaze first to Jenny then back to Rachel.

"We stopped off at Skaggs's on our way back from the mall," Rachel supplied, her tone far more cordial, as if trying to make up for having snapped at him before.

"The mall? You two went shopping?" he asked, his eyebrows lifting to reveal his concern. "And what did you buy?"

"Jenny bought a new pair of running shoes and I bought a new pair of shoestrings for my cleats," Rachel responded quickly, pulling temporarily out of her apprehensive mood. "I got a pair of red-and-white ones like Shelly has—to go with our team colors. We also went by the music store to see what new cassettes had come in, but neither of us bought anything there."

"That's because they didn't have any Bob Seger," mumbled Jenny, hoping to distract Rick from the fact they had spent that time together.

"Sounds like you two made an afternoon of it."

"We did," Rachel admitted. "We also stopped off at Grandma's and watered her plants. Tonight, if she asks me if I remembered to check on them for her, I can tell her I did." She then looked puzzled. "Should I tell her that Grandpa had already watered them or just tell her that I did?"

"Tell her the truth, that you watered them yourself. If she asks you anything about Grandpa, just continue telling her you haven't seen him."

Rachel nodded that she understood.

"Besides, I think your grandmother has already started to realize something is not quite right as far as your grandpa is concerned."

"Why?"

"Because she called the warehouse today wanting to talk with him. When she was told he was not in his office at that moment and asked if she'd rather talk to me instead, she told the receptionist that talking with me would not be necessary and hung up." His eyes dulled with introspection, though he continued to direct his gaze at Rachel. "She's also been questioning Stella Sanford about him, whenever she stops by her room for a quick visit. She and Mrs. Sanford go all the way back to high school, you know."

Remembering Stella Sanford was the stone-faced nurse in ICU, Jenny asked, "And what does Mrs. Sanford tell her?"

"Just that she hasn't seen him in a while. Pretty much what we've asked everyone to say. We don't want anyone purposely lying to her, especially not her friends."

"But what if she comes right out and asks someone?" Jenny asked, aware that was a possibility.

"Then she'll have to be told. If she reaches the point where she knows just what to ask to finally get at the truth, she will pretty well already have figured it out on her own. I just hope Dr. Weathers is around when that happens."

"You sound like you expect it any day," Jenny commented, feeling both hopeful and alarmed.

Although finally remembering that her husband was dead would mean she was getting over her amnesia, Jenny knew it would be terribly painful for her. Like Dr. Weathers had said, when she did remember the truth, it would be like having her husband die all over again. How sad to have to lose someone you love twice.

"The way Mother has been recalling a lot of little details she'd forgotten earlier, I do think it will be any day. And I think that's why she called the warehouse. She's starting to suspect the truth."

Before he could explain further, the telephone rang, causing Rachel to jump at the unexpected sound. Her eyes rounded with hopeful anticipation when she hurriedly scooted her chair away from the table. "I'll get it."

"If it is Sheila or Shelly, don't talk long," Rick cautioned her, glancing at his watch. "We'll be leaving for the hospital in about fifteen or twenty minutes. I'll want you ready."

Jenny's heart hammered wildly, worried that Carla's company had left early. Thinking everything was all about to come to a head, she quickly returned her attention to her plate, not quite ready to face Rick's anger. But when Rachel reentered the room only a few seconds later, her expression clearly disappointed, Jenny knew the caller had not been Carla. She felt the taut muscles across her shoulders and arms slowly relax until they felt almost limp in comparison.

Reprieve, she thought, and silently released the breath she'd held. Then, just as suddenly, she tensed again when she heard Rachel's next words.

"It's for you, Dad. It's Dr. Weathers."

Chapter Ten

"Rachel, Dr. Weathers wants us to get right on over to the hospital," Rick said in a very somber voice when he reentered the dining room after having talked on the telephone in the den for only a few minutes. "Your grandmother knows."

"That Grandpa is dead?" Rachel asked, her face paling with concern. "Who told her?"

"Dr. Weathers did. When he stopped by to check on her a little while ago, she told him that she'd been having tiny flashes of a funeral popping up in the back of her head and wanted to know if the funeral plaguing her had been Dad's. When he told her it very well could have been, she became very emotional. He thinks we need to be with her right now, to help her get over the shock."

Rachel was already pushing her chair back, her eyes glimmering with unshed tears. "I'm ready."

Jenny was in too much emotional chaos to know exactly what she felt when she followed them to the back door. Nor did she know what to say. Instead she stood at the back door and watched, her hands trembling at her sides, while Rick and Rachel hurried toward the garage.

It was nearly nine before they returned, and by that time Jenny was a nervous wreck.

Even though she had known it was too soon, that her birth mother would have to have more time to adjust to the painful memories that had so suddenly returned, every time the telephone rang Jenny had jumped, hoping against hope it would be Rick calling to tell her the time was finally right for her to come to the hospital, but of course that had not happened.

"How'd it go?" she asked, having met them at the back door.

"Pretty well, considering," Rick told her, then reached out to brush her worried cheek reassuringly with the inner curve of his fingers. It was all he could do to comfort her with Rachel still there. And, too, remembering how abruptly Jenny had pulled away from him Saturday night, he knew it was probably all she would allow. If only she felt the same toward him as he did toward her. "Mother has accepted the fact that Dad's dead and she even remembers the night he died of a heart attack. Although her memory is still a little vague in places, she has definitely gotten most of it back."

"She has?" Jenny asked, tingling as much from her own hopeful anticipation as she was from Rick's gentle touch.

"Yes, as far as we can tell," he said, then waited until Rachel had disappeared down the hall and into the den to watch some horror movie that was about to start before he continued in a lower voice so only Jenny could hear.

When he spoke again, the sparkle in his eyes was genuine, because although he still had a few reservations as far as his mother was concerned, he felt Jenny deserved an opportunity to meet her. He knew Jenny would not intentionally do anything to harm their mother and hoped nothing unintentional would happen. "And you'll be pleased to know Dr. Weathers has already said that as soon as Mother has gotten over the intense grief she now feels and is back to her old cheerful self, you will be permitted to meet her. Shouldn't be too long now. Possibly only a matter of weeks."

Weeks? thought Jenny, disheartened at the prospect of having to wait even one more day.

Rick noticed how disappointed she looked and again stroked her cheek gently with the inner curve of his hand, which sent a bewildering array of sensations through her.

"If we weren't so uncertain about the stability of Mother's emotional health right now, we would let you meet her a lot sooner than that. But having just rediscovered Dad's death, she's not up to anything else that could be considered in any way traumatic."

"I know," she said and nodded to show that although she was extremely disappointed, she understood. "Do you think she'll remember having had me when I do finally get to meet her?"

After asking her question, she glanced down at the shiny parquet flooring, not wanting him to know how worried she was, afraid the amnesia might have also affected that part of her memory.

"She already does remember you," he assured her, lifting her chin with the tips of his fingers. A tender smile touched his lips while he searched her troubled brown eyes. "Earlier, Dr. Weathers asked her about several major events in her life, to see if there might be other areas she may have forgotten and he told me she definitely remembering having you."

Jenny was so relieved she felt like crying. Not knowing that much about the unusual type of amnesia her birth mother had, she had worried she might have blocked out that part of her memory as well. Had that proved to be the case, she knew she might never learn what had prompted the decision to put her up for adoption rather than raise her.

"Why? What did she say?" she asked, eager to know more.

Before Rick could fill her in on what the doctor had told him, Jacqueline entered from the kitchen door into the hallway where they stood talking near the back door.

"I'll be going now," she said, looking down to single out the proper key from her key ring. "See you Wednesday."

"Have a good time at your sister's," Rick said, stepping out of the way to let her pass. He waited until she had gone out through the same door he had just entered, then turned back to look at Jenny. "That reminds me. I'll probably be a little late getting home tomorrow evening. I have an appointment at four o'clock to look over a small chain of auto-parts stores that went on the market this week. By the time I've taken a good long look at the two local outlets, then picked up the paperwork they are supposed to have ready for me at both places, it will probably be nearly seven o'clock before I get away. That'll make us late leaving for whatever restaurant Rachel chooses for tomorrow."

Because Tuesdays and Thursdays were Jacqueline's days off, those nights had automatically become family nights out. Before his mother was admitted to the hospital over a month ago, Tuesdays had usually meant supper at his mother's, but that had promptly changed to either sandwiches at home or supper in one of the local restaurants, when it became clear she would be in the hospital for quite some time.

"I guess I'd better go warn Rachel, too," he said, heading toward the den. "I'd hate for her to hurry home after a ball practice only to discover I'm not even going to be here for a while. Besides, she'll need to be thinking of a restaurant where we can be served quickly. I'll want to get back and go over those papers before I meet with the owners again for lunch on Wednesday."

"Wait," Jenny said, hoping to stop him before he entered the den. Knowing it was a very real possibility Rachel would not feel like going out to eat, not if she had discovered the truth about her mother by then, Jenny hurried to intervene. "You don't have to bother with taking us out tomorrow at all. We can plan to have supper here."

"But tomorrow's Jacqueline's day off," he reminded her, thinking she must have forgotten.

"And the perfect opportunity for me to repay some of the kindnesses you and Rachel have shown me since I arrived. Instead of going off to some restaurant, I'll cook supper. That way I can plan it for whatever time you say. It may be a little too hot in June for my specialty, which is homemade Texas chili and corn bread, but I also make a mean pot of spaghetti and a tangy Italian salad dressing that will have you begging for more. The really good thing about spaghetti, the sauce can simmer for hours with no harmful effect and the spaghetti itself only takes about fifteen minutes to cook. I can have everything but the spaghetti ready and we can be eating within twenty minutes after you're home. That will give you just enough time to change and get comfortable."

"But I can't let you do that. You are a guest in this house."

"Only because I was forced on you," she reminded him. "Besides, I'm family. I should pitch in and help. I've loafed around here long enough."

Rick lifted an eyebrow and offered her a truly menacing look when he reminded her, "You are *not* a part of my family. You may be a part of my family's family. But you are not any relation to *me*."

Rather than go into all that again, Jenny put her hands on her hips and questioned. "Are you afraid to eat my cooking?"

"Well, no, but—"

"There'll be no buts about this. I am cooking supper tomorrow night and that, my dear friend, is that!"

"Yes, ma'am," Rick answered dutifully, a playful smile tugging at his mouth, admiring the obstinate streak in her. "As long as you are doing so in the capacity of friendship and not because you still think you are some sort of kin to me. The fact is, the only way you could ever become a true relative of mine is if Mother decided to have you legally declared her daughter or—" His eyebrows rose at the unexpected thought.

"Or what?"

"Or I married you."

"What?" she asked, thinking that preposterous. Brothers and sisters didn't marry. Even if she and Rick were not *legally* kin, they did share the same mother and that made the thought of marriage seem downright ludicrous. Almost as ludicrous as the passionate way she had responded to his kiss the other night. Her cheeks crimsoned at the thought of what had almost happened in that darkened garage. What would people say if they ever found out how she really felt about her biological mother's adopted son?

"I was just thinking aloud," he quickly reassured her, but the smile lingered when he gave what he had said a little more thought. If he ever did decide to remarry, though such an idea had not occurred to him before now, he would want it to be to someone exactly like Jenny, someone who was so very giving of herself, yet not afraid to stand up in support of what she thought was right.

"It doesn't sound to me like you were thinking at all," she commented in a teasing tone, then tilted her head to one side, enjoying the alluring shape of his smile and the endearing sparkle in his translucent blue eyes. "But, then, rational thinking does not seem to be a trait that runs in the family, does it?"

"Whose family might that be? Mine or yours?" he asked, lowering one dark blond eyebrow with clear warning.

"Never mind," she said, thinking it was time to steer the conversation onto something a little less perplexing. "Just as long as it has been decided that I will cook tomorrow's supper."

When Rachel learned what Jenny planned to do about supper, she immediately volunteered to help. Later, when Jenny stopped by the den to tell her goodnight, she admitted the real reason she was so eager to help was because she felt so grateful to Jenny for having given her the courage to call her mother. She was very excited about the telephone call still to come, and when Rick ducked his head in only a few minutes later to tell Rachel it was time for her to be off to bed, she convinced him she was too captivated by the movie she was watching to give it up.

"Then record it and finish watching it in the morning," he suggested. "You need your sleep."

"But that's just it. I couldn't possibly sleep until I know for certain that the monster who's been murdering everyone is dead."

Rick sighed, then remembering how many late nights he had put in watching horror flicks on television during his teen years, he relented. "Okay, but as soon as this one movie is over, you get on up to bed. I've already locked the doors, so all you have to do is remember to turn out all the lights and hit the sack."

When Jenny followed Rick from the room, Rachel was sitting on the sofa beside the telephone pretending to be deeply engrossed in an action scene filled with growls, groans and lung-collapsing screams.

Finding sleep impossible, though not because she worried there was some evil monster on the prowl, Jenny waited until a little after midnight, then slipped from the bedroom and went first to Rachel's room, then downstairs to learn what had happened. She found Rachel sound asleep on the sofa, the telephone on the floor beside her, her hand dangling just inches above.

A sharp pain pierced Jenny's heart when she realized Carla had never called, and Rachel had obviously stayed awake for as long as she possibly could, waiting for the telephone to ring so she could catch it before her father did.

Tiptoeing gently into the room, Jenny turned off the television, then walked over to where Rachel lay curled on the sofa, hugging a throw pillow beneath her chin. Knowing the child should not sleep on the sofa all night, Jenny considered carrying her upstairs. But judging by the girl's size and the distance she would have to carry her, she decided it would be better for both of them to wake her.

"Rachel, time to get on up to bed," she said, shaking the girl's shoulder gently, just enough to rouse her.

"Why? What time is it?" Rachel asked, forcing her eyes open and frowning questioningly when she realized she was still in the den.

"Almost twelve-thirty. You were supposed to be in bed over an hour ago."

Rachel swung her legs over and blinked with confusion when her foot hit the telephone. Her eyes then widened with sudden realization and she came immediately alert.

When she looked at Jenny then, it was with the saddest blue eyes Jenny had ever seen.

"Mom never called."

"I gathered," Jenny said, angry with the woman for having failed to fulfill her promise to return a simple telephone call. "Maybe her guests didn't leave until very late and she was afraid you'd be in bed."

"But I told her I'd be awake," Rachel said, her face so full of disappointment, Jenny immediately put an arm around her shoulders to comfort her.

"But that was when you both thought it would be around eleven. It could very well have been midnight before they all left. Or it might be that a few of them are still there even now. Some people never know when it's time to go home."

Rachel pressed her cheek against Jenny's shoulder. "I guess I'll just have to wait and try calling her again in the morning."

"And in the meantime you need to go upstairs, climb into your own bed and get some sleep. You'll want to be wide-awake and alert when you talk to your mother tomorrow."

Aware there was no reason to protest, Rachel stumbled to her feet while Jenny put the telephone back where it belonged.

"I'll see you in the morning," she mumbled, then headed directly for the door, her shoulders slumped and her arms hanging limply at her sides.

Jenny stayed long enough to put the pillows back in place and turn out the light before following. She stopped by Rachel's room long enough to make sure the girl had indeed gone on to bed, then returned to her bedroom, so annoyed with Rachel's mother she still could not sleep.

When she first arrived in Tyler, Jenny had wisely cautioned herself against becoming too emotionally involved with these people—these different members of her birth mother's family. She knew she would only see them but a few times, and there was no reason to become all that attached to them. But like it or not, she had obviously not heeded her own forewarnings because she had definitely gotten herself involved. Deeply involved.

Although she had not wanted to, she cared about Rachel and Rick, and she cared about what happened to them. She cared enough to wish she could help them through the different problems they had. And cared enough to dread leaving them, though she had known from the beginning leaving was inevitable. She was not truly a part of their lives. And never would be. And when the time came for her to leave, she would be easily forgotten.

Why hadn't she kept her emotions under better control? Why had she allowed herself to fall so deeply in love with these strangers? Having allowed her heart to become that involved would do nothing but bring her pain when the time finally came for her to return to Stockfield.

Just the thought of leaving, of having to be away from Rick and Rachel and eventually being out of their thoughts as well, hurt Jenny tremendously, making it impossible for her to fall asleep until well after three. When the alarm went off barely three hours later, it felt as if someone had crept into her room and clubbed her over the head. She had a difficult time coming awake and felt a dull ache near the back of her neck.

When she went downstairs to have breakfast with Rick a few minutes after seven, she was surprised to find Rachel there, too. Since her arrival, Rachel had not once wakened in time to share breakfast with them.

"My, my, aren't you the early bird," Jenny commented when she entered the room, wondering what Rick had thought when Rachel had appeared so early.

"She said she wanted to be sure to be up in time to help you in the kitchen," Rick said, looking somewhat perplexed while he watched Jenny take her usual seat to his left. "I told her you probably wouldn't even start on supper until sometime this afternoon, but she said she didn't want to take any chances."

"I want to learn how to make homemade spaghetti," Rachel said, coming in ready defense of herself, though it did nothing to fool Jenny.

Jenny knew the real reason Rachel had risen early was because she wanted to try calling her mother again and had realized she would have to make that call fairly early if she wanted to catch her before she left for work.

"Well, you'll certainly be learning from the best," Jenny commented and winked while she reached for the nearest cereal box. Because she liked most breakfast cereals, it really did not matter to her what brand was inside. "My spaghetti sauce rivals that of famous Italian chefs worldwide."

"Aren't we lucky to have someone like you," Rick teased, reaching forward to pat her hand lightly. "I just hope you know how greatly you are appreciated."

Jenny's whole arm tingled as a result of his playful touch and when she looked at him then, she saw more than a brotherly interest glimmering in his eyes. Quivering to the bone, she quickly looked away and reached immediately for the milk. "I just hope you continue to say such kind things after you've actually tasted my cooking." Much less after he had learned what she'd done to encourage Rachel to call her mother.

"Are you saying you may have exaggerated your expertise?" he asked while he tore apart one of the two breakfast muffins he had just put on his plate.

"Maybe a little," she admitted, then shook off the apprehensive feeling that had crept over her, knowing his good mood would not last. "But not much. I am a pretty good cook."

Rachel was too busy shoveling spoonfuls of cereal into her mouth to comment, but she nodded as if to confirm her confidence in Jenny. She then reached for one of the muffins and tore it in half, preparing to plop the whole section into her mouth.

"Good to see your appetite has returned," Rick commented, watching while she popped the large piece of muffin into her mouth. "Maybe I should have microwaved that entire package of muffins."

Aware Rachel was eating as much to quell her nervous energy as she was from hunger, Jenny teased. "Better yet, you should've gone out for chocolate-covered doughnuts. Seems we both have a weakness when it comes to those."

Again Rachel nodded that she quite agreed, but this time she managed to clear her mouth with a quick swallow of milk in time to comment. "The more chocolate the better." She glanced at the clock on the buffet then at her father, her forehead knitted with concern. "Shouldn't you be going? It's almost seven-thirty."

Rick glanced up from having just buttered his muffin, his expression surprised. "Are you trying to get rid of me?"

Rachel immediately looked back at her plate. "No. I just didn't want you to be late."

"Well, you're right. I do need to get going. Today will be a very busy day. Remember I will probably be late, so don't expect to eat until at least seven or later." Having said that, he pushed his chair back, then stood. "Just don't you two do anything I wouldn't do while I'm gone."

Jenny and Rachel exchanged quick glances, but tried not to reveal their apprehension. They waited until he had left the room before slowly releasing mutually held breaths.

"I thought he'd never leave," Rachel commented, glowering at the chair her father had vacated. "He used to be out the door by seven-fifteen."

Jenny's eyebrows lifted curiously at such a comment, because she hadn't known him to leave until at least seven-thirty and sometimes it was nearly eight before he was finally on his way. Was she in some way delaying his departure every morning? Did he resent her for that? Somehow she didn't think so. For some reason, she believed he truly enjoyed the time they spent together every morning.

Rachel waited until they had heard the car drive off before rising from the table.

Knowing Jacqueline was gone, Jenny immediately began to clear the table, but she willingly put aside the stack of dirty dishes to go with Rachel into the den and be with her when she conducted the second telephone call. While she watched Rachel make herself comfortable on the sofa, she hoped Carla would be home so Rachel could get the worst of her dilemma behind her.

Surprisingly, Rachel seemed more determined than tense when she quickly punched in the telephone number and waited for the first ring. It wasn't until someone had actually answered that her eyes widened with sudden concern and her chest filled with a deep anticipating breath.

"Hello, Mom? This is Rachel again. How come you didn't call last night like you said you would?"

There was a short pause during which Rachel's expression remained extremely cautious while she focused on nothing in particular.

"No, I understand, and you're right. Dad would have had a fit if you'd phoned after midnight. But the main reason I called you last night was because—"

There was another short pause during which Rachel's expression went from cautiously apprehensive to clearly disappointed, but her voice remained clear of any emotion and Jenny was proud of her for that.

"Sure, Mom, I understand—no, I'll be here. I'm going to be helping Jenny make spaghetti this afternoon. No, Jacqueline hasn't quit. Jenny's a friend of Grandma's. She's staying with us for a few days until Grandma gets well enough to have non-family visitors."

Rachel's expression temporarily went from disappointed to amused when she glanced over at Jenny. "No, she's not old, and we're not having to put up with her. She's a lot of fun to be around. What? Oh, about your age, I guess. Sure, she's pretty. No, in the guest room down the hall. Okay. No, I understand. Talk to you then.''

Rachel stared at the telephone for several seconds after having replaced the receiver in its cradle, as if trying to decide what she thought about the outcome of the call. Finally she looked at Jenny and explained, ''She was on her way out. She told me she'd make a special note in her appointment book to remember to call me during lunch. But she said she usually doesn't eat until about one or one-thirty.''

''And why didn't she call last night?''

''Just like you thought. One of her friends didn't leave until way after midnight and she was afraid she'd make Dad mad if she called that late. So now I have to wait until this afternoon to talk with her.''

But afternoon came and there was no telephone call. By five o'clock Rachel was so restless Jenny suggested she try calling again. Thinking Carla probably hadn't had time to get home from work yet, they were both surprised when she answered on the very first ring.

''Hello, Mom? Me, again. I thought you were going to call me today.''

The pain and horror that filled Rachel at that moment made Jenny rush forward and kneel before her. She frowned while searching Rachel's face for more indication of what had been said.

''No, Mom, I don't want any money from you. Yes, I know I'm supposed to get that from Dad. I just wanted to talk to you. I thought maybe you and I could—''

She swallowed hard, her lower lip trembling visibly by now. ''I didn't know.'' Her voice wavered, revealing how badly she was hurt. "I just wanted to talk to you is all. I—I'm sorry."

She listened a few seconds longer, then breathed out a painful goodbye. She sat curled on the sofa, cradling the receiver in her hands, unable to think clearly enough to hang it up.

Gently Jenny took the receiver from her and replaced it on the base.

"What happened?" she asked in a soft voice aware the foolish woman had done or said something to hurt her daughter terribly.

"I made her mad," Rachel said in a barely audible voice. "She was expecting an important telephone call from her boyfriend and got mad when it was me instead." Tears filled her eyes and her face drew into such a pinched, agony-filled expression, Jenny didn't think she could bear it. She reached for her hands and held them between her own.

"Mom thought I was calling because I wanted money. It never occurred to her that I might be calling because I've missed her and just wanted to see her."

"Oh, Rachel, I'm so sorry," Jenny said and quickly gathered the girl into her arms. She felt Rachel's shoulders quake when she began to sob openly.

"Sh-she told me to get o-off the phone so her boyfriend could call. Sh-she doesn't want me calling back, either."

Jenny could not imagine anyone being quite that heartless, and wondered how Rick could ever have become involved with a woman like that. "Maybe she had a bad day and you happened to call at the exact wrong moment."

Rachel refused to comment. All she could do was continue to weep uncontrollably against Jenny's shoulder.

Gently Jenny stroked her blond hair and let her cry to her heart's content. When finally the tears subsided, she pushed the girl away just far enough to be able to look into her tear-dampened eyes.

"Are you going to be okay?" she asked, wondering how long it would take her to put everything together in her mind and come up with something positive.

"Yeah, I'll live," Rachel said, wiping her nose with the back of her wrist then forcing a brief smile. "I've gotten along without her this long, I guess I can get along without her some more."

"And remember you still have me," Jenny said, all the while feeling guilty over the knowledge she would not be there forever. Rick had been right about one thing. When the time came for her to leave, Rachel would be very hurt. How that made her heart wrench. Rachel had suffered enough. "And what's more, you still have your father. Despite what you may think, he loves you very much."

Rachel sat quietly while she let that remark soak in. "And I still have Shelly and Sheila," she added, just as eager to find a bright spot in her suddenly dismal situation. "And I still have Grandma."

"So why are you so teary-eyed?" Jenny wanted to know. "Your mother may be too busy for you right now, but you still have the rest of us and we have plenty of time for you."

Rachel thrust her chin forward, in much the same proud manner as her father would have in a similar situation. "Yeah, why *am* I so teary-eyed? I've got more friends than I'll ever need."

Having said that, she rose from the couch and headed proudly for the door. "We'd better go check on your spaghetti sauce before it burns. I'd hate to serve Dad burned spaghetti."

Although Jenny realized Rachel's heartbreak was far from over, the counselor in her knew that now was not the time to discuss it. Rachel needed the opportunity to adjust to the painful realization her mother was not as she had remembered her to be, and Jenny was very willing to give that time.

That night Rick was surprised to learn that Rachel had missed softball practice, and when he noticed how subdued she behaved during supper and how very little spaghetti she ate, he concluded she was ill.

"I think I'd better call Dr. Weathers and ask him to stop by and check on you on his way home," he commented, wanting only to help.

"But I'm not sick," Rachel assured him, but her voice held so little conviction it hardly convinced her father.

"We won't know that until he has checked you." He set his napkin aside in preparation of making the telephone call.

"But I'm *not* sick," Rachel yelled, this time with tears in her eyes. "Can't you understand a statement as simple as that? I am not sick."

Rick was so startled by her emotional outburst he sat speechless while she pushed her chair back and ran from the room.

"What was that all about?" he asked, still staring dumbfounded at the door where she had disappeared.

Jenny knew she risked alienating him forever but decided he should know the truth. "She spoke with her mother this afternoon."

"Where?" Rick wanted to know, looking suddenly alarmed. His lean jaw turned granite-hard.

"On the telephone. Rachel called to see if she might be allowed to visit her in Longview sometime soon."

The muscles in Rick's face worked furiously. "And I gather Carla told her no."

"Rachel never got to ask. Carla was so upset for her having called that she never even gave Rachel a chance to explain her reason for having done so."

Rick shook his head, his face filled with a stark combination of anger and misery. "What could possibly have possessed that girl to call her? I thought I had her convinced to let me do all the telephoning."

Jenny took a deep breath, held it for only a second, then answered truthfully. "I suggested it."

When Rick turned his head to look at her then, his expression was unreadable. It was only the tone of his voice that suggested his strong feeling of betrayal. "*You* suggested it? Why on earth would you do that?"

"I thought it was time Rachel learned the truth about her mother."

"That was not up to you to decide."

"Maybe not, but that doesn't change the fact that I am the one who encouraged her to call."

"But why?" He looked deeply into her eyes, as if truly wanting to understand.

Jenny clasped her hands together in her lap and fought the urge to look away. "I wanted her to see that *you* were not the reason her mother stayed away."

"Me? Why would she think I had anything to do with Carla's absence? What reason could I possibly have?"

"She'd decided it was because you were jealous of Carla, jealous enough to want to keep them apart."

"That's ridiculous."

"Maybe so, but it is how she felt. By having made all those flimsy excuses for Carla, you had inadvertently made yourself out to be the eventual fall guy. Evidently you had told her that Carla had been sick lately, yet Rachel knew for a fact that was not true. Shelly and Sheila had both seen Carla at the mall not too long ago, and Carla looked quite healthy then."

"But she *is* sick," Rick muttered, in ready defense of himself. "In the head. She'd have to be not to want to see Rachel."

"I agree. And I think she probably needs serious counseling, but that was something Rachel had to find out for herself. If I had tried to tell her, or especially if you had tried to tell her the truth, she wouldn't have believed it. She wouldn't have *wanted* to believe it. Until now, she has always thought of her mother as someone who was always there for her."

"That was hardly the case. When Carla wasn't at one of her fancy club meetings or at the country club playing a few rounds of golf, she was off shopping somewhere. She rarely stayed home."

"But evidently she took Rachel with her sometimes, because Rachel fondly remembers having gone shopping with her mother and eating lunch with her mother and her friends.''

"But that was only on Jacqueline's days off, when Carla didn't have anybody else to keep Rachel,'' Rick commented, his tone bitter.

"Still, Rachel remembered her the way she wanted to remember her. She needed to find out the truth, and she needed to do it on her own.''

While Rick sat tapping his fingers against the table, as if trying to decide what his final judgment of the matter might be, Jenny waited, her stomach so tied in knots she could barely breath.

"Why didn't you tell me what you had done?'' he asked, clearly trying to understand.

"Because you would have tried to stop her from calling and she would have viewed your actions as another attempt to keep her and her mother apart. It would have undermined everything I was trying to accomplish.''

"And did you accomplish what you set out to accomplish?''

"It's really too soon to tell,'' Jenny admitted. "After it was all over and her mother had made it perfectly clear she no longer wanted any part of her, I quickly reminded Rachel that she still had you. She didn't attempt to argue that point with me, which I think was a good sign.''

Rick sat thinking about all he had just learned, giving no indication how he felt.

"Are you angry with me?'' she finally found the courage to ask. She had to know.

"Yes,'' he said, nodding vacantly, then when he noticed her pained expression, he quickly reached forward to take her hand. "But I'll get over it." He dampened his lips with his tongue while he contemplated the matter further. "I just hope Rachel finds a way to recover as quickly as I do."

Chapter Eleven

That night, after Rick had more time to think about what Jenny had done, he realized how difficult it must have been for her. Knowing how deeply Jenny cared for Rachel, the decision to encourage his daughter to make such a volatile telephone call could not have been an easy one to make.

Although personally he would have handled the situation differently, he was impressed with what she had done nonetheless. He was also impressed with the time she had been willing to spend with Rachel, helping make up for the immeasurable pain Carla had so thoughtlessly caused.

While he had taken to his room to go over the reports he had brought home, Jenny and Rachel had spent the rest of their evening in Rachel's bedroom writing letters to friends and discussing their favorite rock groups, the sort of things Rachel usually did with her younger friends.

Not only was Rick impressed with how willing Jenny was to help ease Rachel's pain, he was also impressed with how easily Jenny had put her own needs aside for the sake of their mother's well-being. She was generous beyond belief.

Despite the fact that Jenny had not yet been allowed to meet the woman she so dearly longed to see, she had not pressed for an early meeting. Even though waiting until Dr. Weathers declared their mother physically and emotionally well enough to meet with her might make Jenny late in returning to work, she had agreed to wait until the doctor finally gave his okay. She had done nothing to force the issue.

Although the only information Jenny acquired about her biological mother thus far had come from the stories he and Rachel had provided in the course of regular conversation, Jenny had not returned to the hospital since the day they had gone there together and learned about their mother's sudden relapse. She had promised to stay away, and she had. Despite a very strong desire to see the woman, she had not tried to force her way into her hospital room. That alone was commendable.

Truth was, everything about Jenny Ryan impressed Rick. She was smart, beautiful and caring. If only she would get over the strange uneasiness she felt over being his "almost" sister and realize that he longed for more than sisterly affection from her. Yet no matter how he tried to convince her that they were not truly related, that they were free to develop a deeper sort of relationship, she clung to the inconsequential fact that they shared the same mother, almost as if it was a shield of some sort.

It occurred to him then that perhaps Jenny was afraid to give their relationship a chance. Perhaps she was afraid she might fall in love with him, afraid she would be hurt again in much the same way she had been hurt by that selfish dimwit she'd been married to before.

If only she could see that not all men were like that. *He* was not like that. He was not the type to decide suddenly he would rather have someone else simply because he was bored. Once he made a commitment to someone or to something, he stuck by it, just as he would stick by her if she were ever to fall in love with him.

His blood heated at the vivid memory of the kiss he had stolen in the garage three nights before. If only she hadn't suddenly decided to pull away as she had. If only she had allowed herself to explore the strong feelings developing between them. But she hadn't, and he certainly had no intention of forcing her.

He would have to wait until the time was more suitable and try again.

If he could survive the wait.

At the same time Rick lay awake in his bed, trying to sort through the odd type of relationship that had developed between them, Jenny lay in her bed, aware she too felt something unusually strong whenever she was with Rick. Although she was still convinced a relationship between them could never work, and was still very self-conscious of the fact they shared the same mother, though in entirely different ways, Jenny could think of nothing else but what it would be like to share an intimate relationship with him.

Despite the fact she'd gotten so little rest the night before, worrying the way she had about what would happen when at last Rachel did talk with her mother, Jenny was still unable to get any sleep. Her body was so tired her arms felt weighted at her sides, but her brain was wide-awake and refused to shut down for the night.

Despite her desire not to think about Rick, Jenny also wondered what might have happened that previous Saturday night if she hadn't pulled away from him when she did. If, instead, she had allowed nature to take its course.

Her whole body tingled when she realized that even though there had been three teenage girls in the house at the time, she and Rick could have easily ended up in bed together, quietly but passionately making love.

She grimaced when she realized how thrilling she found the thought. Although falling in love with Rick or with anyone definitely did not fit into her plans, she was afraid it might have already happened.

When she had left for Tyler, her only purpose had been to meet her birth mother, find out something about her beginnings and return home. She had not planned to become attached to anyone. Yet there she was, unable to think of little else but how wonderful it had felt to be in the arms of her biological mother's adopted son.

She moaned softly, more aware than ever that such a relationship would never work. If only what she felt for him was not already so much a part of her. If only she could leave there when the time came and never think of him again. But that was asking the impossible.

Rick's handsome image had already been permanently burned into her brain. She would never be able to forget him, nor would she be able to forget the strong feelings she had for him. Nor would she be able to forget Rachel, who so needed a caring woman in her life right now.

It was quite a predicament. The only thing she could possibly hope to do to help save the situation from becoming any worse was *not* react upon her innermost feelings. As long as she did not allow what she felt for Rick and Rachel to alter her actions in any way, she was safe.

But even that seemed hopeless. Ever since she had met Rick, and they had begun spending so much time together, she had started having wild, tantalizing fantasies involving him. Fantasies that had left her breathless and wide-eyed at times when she should have been sleeping. And even when she did manage finally to fall asleep, he came to her in her dreams, trying even then to convince her they were not really related.

Covering her head with the extra pillow, as if that might in some way help smother his handsome image right out of her brain, Jenny again moaned aloud. After the cruel way Robert had treated her, she had vowed never to become that involved with or that committed to anyone again, especially anyone as strong-willed and as determined that things go his way as he had been.

Therefore, it was bewildering to catch herself actually daydreaming about sharing an intimate relationship with someone just like him, someone every bit as strong-willed and every bit as determined—if not *more* so. Her pulses throbbed at the mere thought.

"JENNY, I THINK we need to talk," Rick said barely seconds after he had entered her bedroom the following morning.

Because it had been so late before she had finally fallen asleep and because she hadn't remembered to set the alarm, Jenny had overslept and missed breakfast. She was startled to discover it was after eight when she had finally realized there was persistent knocking on her door.

"What about?" she asked, tucking the turquoise-blue cotton blouse she'd so hurriedly donned into the same jeans she had worn the night before.

"About us," he responded, noticing her slender waist while she adjusted her clothing. "About the fact that I want us to be more than just friends."

Jenny's brown eyes widened and her hands froze in their task. A fiery sense of panic cascaded over her. She had not yet come to terms with her feelings for him, therefore she did not want to be told that he might have similar feelings for her. "Then perhaps we should wait and discuss it tonight after Rachel goes off to sleep."

Thinking that might be better, knowing it would give them more time to discuss the matter, he nodded. "Okay, tonight it is. But just be sure you understand, I do intend for us to talk about this tonight. I won't be put off any longer."

Jenny watched, her eyes still as round as saucers, when he then turned and stalked from the room. Her forehead creased into a puzzled frown when she realized he had seemed almost angry with her. She wondered if he still held a grudge for what she had done the day before.

She was so worried about what Rick planned to discuss with her that evening, Jenny was not even aware when Rachel woke up hours later. Immersed in thought, it wasn't until Rachel had entered the room where Jenny was trying futilely to concentrate on a novel she had started earlier during the week that she was aware the girl had come downstairs.

"Have you had breakfast?" Jenny asked, glancing at the clock and realizing it was nearly time for lunch.

"No. I'm not hungry yet," Rachel said, then came forward to sit beside her on the sofa. "I wanted to ask you something."

Aware of Rachel's pensive mood, Jenny immediately set her book aside and gave the girl her full attention. "What is it?"

Rachel's face twisted into a peculiar expression, as if she was not quite sure how to word what it was she wanted to ask. "I've been thinking about the way Mom treated me on the phone yesterday and the way Dad had been treating me lately—" She paused again, still trying to find the right words to express herself.

"And?" Jenny encouraged.

"And I was wondering what you thought."

"About which?"

"About the way Dad has been trying to keep me and Mom apart. Do you think maybe it had nothing to do with him being jealous? Do you think maybe he *knew* she might treat me like that?"

"Yes, I think he knew. And I think in his own way he believed he was protecting you."

"But why? Why didn't he just tell me the truth?"

"Because he was afraid the truth would hurt you too much," Jenny said, then bent forward to meet

Rachel's perplexed gaze. "It may not have been the best way to handle the situation, but your father was hoping to spare you the pain he knew you would feel when you first found out that your mother had renounced everyone from her former life, even you."

"But why did she do that? What did we ever do to her that was so awful?"

"I personally don't think it was anything either of you did, but for some very real reason your mother decided she wants a whole new life and doesn't seem to care whom she hurts or what she has to do to get that new life. Although your father does not, nor do I fully understand why your mother has decided she needs such a complete change in her life, we do know that she has cut herself off from everyone she knew before—even her friends."

"So Dad was protecting me?"

"That's what he thought. But there was no way he could protect you from something like that forever. Eventually you had to discover the truth."

Rachel sat back, lost in thought for a moment, then asked, "Did you know about my mom when you suggested I call?"

Jenny refused to lie to the girl. "Yes, Rachel, I did. But I thought it was time you discovered the truth before your relationship with your father became any worse."

Rachel looked at her for a second, then glanced off into the distance again. "So you pretty well knew what Mom was going to say to me."

"No. I had no idea what she would say," Jenny corrected. "I think, deep down, I'd hoped she would hear your voice and realize how much she missed you.

I had hoped that would make her come to her senses before it was too late. I don't think she realizes what she risks losing. I think she is just so wrapped up in establishing this new life she wants so badly that she hasn't thought ahead to how empty that new life will be without any family at all.''

"You don't have a family, do you?"

Jenny's eyebrows arched while she tried to decide how to answer that. "My parents died a couple of years ago in a very serious accident and I was never fortunate enough to have a brother or sister. I do have a couple of great aunts and a few distant cousins who live in Wisconsin, but I rarely get to see them.''

"And you already told me you don't have any children,'' Rachel remembered. "That means your life is pretty empty right now, doesn't it?"

Until she had come to Tyler and met Rick and Rachel, Jenny wouldn't have believed her life at all empty, but now she wasn't so sure. "I have lots of friends."

"So do I, but I wouldn't like to think of what my life would be like without Dad and Grandma.''

Jenny felt encouraged by that remark. "Then you have started to forgive your father for having kept the truth from you?"

"Yeah, I guess so,'' she conceded. "I think you are probably right. He was doing what he thought was best for me. Just like you thought you were doing what was best for me when you encouraged me to call.''

At that moment the telephone rang, bringing their conversation to a temporary halt while Rachel leaned over to answer it.

"It's for you. Some lady named Carole."

Jenny's eyes widened with immediate alarm, wondering what had happened to make Carole call in the middle of the day like that. Carole was the type who usually waited for the lower nighttime or weekend rates.

"Hello?"

"Hi, Jen, how's it going?"

"Pretty good," she answered in a tentative tone.

"Met your mother yet?"

"No, not yet, but it should only be a few more weeks before I do."

"That's one of the reasons I called. I went by the high-school office to get an address I needed and noticed that you are posted to be back here July 9. I asked Karrisa what would happen if you were a couple of weeks late, and she said Howard would probably be pulling hair. There are already over fifty requests for schedule changes, and on top of that almost forty new students have moved into the neighborhood. Plus you still have all those freshmen to schedule. I really don't think they can let you put off getting started any later than the ninth."

"But I have to stay until the doctor says she's well enough to be told about me. I promised." Her heart ached at the thought of returning home without having succeeded in her original quest.

"Well, you'd better find some way to speed things up down there, because Karissa told me that Howard has mentioned calling you and asking you to come in sooner than the ninth. He doesn't want it to end up like last year. Remember how this place turned into a last-minute madhouse?"

"Do they know where I am?"

"Not precisely, but they know I know where you are. Maybe you'd better give the high school a call and see what you can work out. I'd hate for you to lose your job over this. Who would I have to trade gossip with, if you left?"

"I'm sure you'd find someone," Jenny commented with a chuckle. "Okay, I'll give them a call before three and explain my situation, but there's little chance I can be back before the ninth—if then."

"You know if they fire you it's the same as having fired me, too. We'll both be looking for a new high school." She paused while she thought about that. "Hmm, I wonder if there are any openings for counselors and phys-ed teachers in Hawaii."

"With your complexion? You'd have a permanent sunburn," Jenny said, laughing. "Besides, you know you can't possibly leave Texas. It's too much a part of you."

"How right you are, partner," Carole quipped in her worst Texas drawl. "Just remember to call me after you've talked to Howard, so I can know if we'll be looking for new jobs or not."

When Jenny hung up the telephone she was smiling. It had been good to hear Carole's voice, even if the news she'd brought was not the best.

"Who was that?" Rachel wanted to know, looking at her peculiarly.

"A friend I work with. She wanted to warn me that I may be asked to come back to work earlier than the ninth."

"Does that mean you'll be leaving soon?" Rachel asked, her face filled with instant concern.

"Not for a couple of weeks yet. They may want me there before the ninth, but I doubt I'll be able to get there any sooner. I promised to stay until your grandmother was well enough to have other visitors and I still hope to do just that."

"I don't understand why you can't just go and see Grandma now. Mrs. Sanford goes every day, and so do several of her other friends," Rachel pointed out. "I don't see why you can't go in to see her, too."

Jenny shifted uncomfortably. "Maybe it is because too many of her friends are coming to see her. Maybe Dr. Weathers thinks she isn't up to seeing any more people than she already is."

Rachel shrugged. "Still, it seems unfair to make you wait. But, then, once Dr. Weathers finds out you have to get back because of your job, maybe he'll find a way to keep some of those other women away long enough to fit you in there somewhere."

Glad Rachel had accepted such a flimsy excuse, Jenny nodded. "Maybe so."

Rachel remained quiet for several more seconds before her face twisted into another pensive frown. "Will you be coming back to visit Grandma again very soon?"

"I hope so," Jenny answered honestly. "I hope to be able to come see her regularly from now on."

Rachel's expression brightened a little. "And will you come by to see me, too?"

"Of course, I will. And who knows, maybe you can come to visit me from time to time."

"Maybe," Rachel conceded, then twisted her mouth into a wistful smile. "Wouldn't it be nice if you could stay here forever?"

Jenny also smiled at the thought. "Yes, it would be nice. But my job and my friends are way on the other side of Texas. Plus I have my own house there, and a dog who misses me." Though not much, as long as Carole was stopping by regularly to feed him, she mused. Walter's loyalties always lay with whoever was supplying the food. "Although I'd love to stay here for a long, long time, I do have responsibilities back home."

"Still, I wish you could stay," Rachel said, then rose from the sofa and sauntered aimlessly out of the room.

By evening, when Rick returned home, Jenny had already called and talked to Howard and had been told that he did indeed want her to come in a few days early to turn in the figures for the preliminary budget and start on the upcoming schedules. When she had then explained the situation to him, he had sounded truly sympathetic, but had told her quite frankly if she couldn't make it back by at least the ninth, he would be forced to look for an immediate replacement. Matters had gotten well out of hand since she'd left. An unusual number of students had already requested schedule changes and the school was having to eliminate all but one Spanish II class since there had been so little interest in it, which meant even more schedule changes. He had also mentioned that twice the number of new students had contacted his office thus far, wanting to know when they could preregister.

Aware of the problems her being away could cause, Jenny had promised either to be there on the ninth or to telephone him a few days prior to let him know she would not make it in time and would therefore understand if he chose to replace her. Although her job was important to her, it not as important as finally meeting her biological mother. She could always find a new place to work, but it was possible she would have only the one opportunity to meet her birth mother.

If the woman suffered another sudden relapse, and it proved as bad as her earlier relapses, Jenny knew this might be her only opportunity to meet the woman who had given birth to her—and her only chance to find out who her biological father had been and why they had decided to give her up for adoption.

Missing such a critical opportunity to talk to her birth mother was not a risk Jenny wanted to take. She had said she would stay until she was finally allowed to meet the woman who had given her birth, and she had meant it. She just hoped it occurred before the ninth.

Even though she knew telling Rick about what had happened would in no way affect when she would be allowed to finally meet her birth mother, Jenny thought she should tell him what she had found out anyway. He deserved to know what had happened.

"I talked with the principal at the high school where I work today," she said while they were sitting outside on the shaded portion of the patio waiting for Jacqueline to announce supper.

"Howard?" he asked, that name having stuck in his memory. He felt a cold wave of apprehension when he realized they had probably discussed the date she was expected to return to West Texas. "What did he have to say?"

"He told me I am scheduled to be back to work on July 9, which is about when I thought it would be. He then tried to convince me to come in earlier, around the first, but I explained to him that there was very little chance I'd be allowed to meet my biological mother before then. I told him the best I could do was try to be there by the ninth."

"But that's only two weeks away," he complained, feeling a sudden constriction inside his chest. He now had only two weeks to convince her to give them a chance.

"I know it's only two weeks," Jenny said, her eyes rounded with concern. "That's why I hope our mother gets better very quickly. The way Howard made it sound, I won't have any free time until early August, and then only if I've finished with the entire freshman class, which is not likely."

"How much free time would you have if you did finish?"

"Probably just a few days, which tacked on to a weekend would give me enough time to drive over for a quick visit, but it's not definite I'll get those few days."

"When would be your next chance to come?"

"Thanksgiving. Although technically I am supposed to have Labor Day off, it's too close to the opening of school, when there comes a whole new wave of scheduling problems. I usually end up working through that holiday just to keep my head above water."

"What if I were to find you a job here locally," Rick suggested, trying to think of anything that might keep her there. "We have two high schools right here in

Tyler, and dozens of others within easy commuting distance."

Jenny felt a surge of exhilaration over the thought of moving to East Texas, but realized he had suggested the job change because he still hoped to convince her to change her mind about him. He still longed for a deeper relationship than what was shared between brother and sister. But nothing had happened to change her belief than a closer relationship just wouldn't work between them. It would be asking for more trouble than either of them could handle.

"I appreciate the offer, but I think I'd better stay right where I am. Besides, my best friend, Carole, would have a fit if I bailed out on her now. And, too, our mother might not like the thought of having me live quite that close. She might prefer I stay in my own part of Texas." Eager to steer the conversation toward something else, before they veered onto the very discussion he had wanted to have early that morning, she quickly added, "And speaking of our mother, why haven't you said anything about her today? Didn't you go by to see her this morning, as you'd planned?"

"I went this afternoon," he answered, aware he was being manipulated away from the more personal conversation but not ready to make an issue of it. "She seemed much better. She still gets a little teary-eyed whenever we talk about Dad, but I think she had accepted it rather well."

"Well enough to be told about me?" Jenny asked. Her heart pounded rapidly at the thought.

Both Jenny and Rick were so immersed in their conversation, neither noticed that Rachel had stepped outside to tell them supper was ready, therefore neither bothered to speak in lower tones while continuing the discussion.

After padding across the brick in her bare feet, Rachel stopped just a few yards away, waiting for them to stop talking long enough to be interrupted.

"That's not for me to say," Rick answered with a slow shake of his head. "Dr. Weathers will have to be the one to decide when Mother is well enough to be told that the daughter she put up for adoption so many years ago has returned and is eager to meet her."

"But do you think that will be anytime soon?" Jenny pressed, knowing he was her only link to that sort of information.

"Shouldn't be long," he admitted, though in truth he wished it would be months yet—for his own sake. Although he didn't hope his mother's grief lingered any longer than was necessary, he did secretly hope that Dr. Weathers would put off letting Jenny meet her for as long as possible, anything to keep Jenny right where she was. "Tell you what I'll do. I'll ask Dr. Weathers how much longer he thinks it will be, if I see him when Rachel and I go at nine. He should have a pretty good idea how long it will be before she's ready to be confronted by her past."

"You make it sound as if I'm out to cause trouble," Jenny said, frowning. "You know that's not true. I just want to meet her. I want to know the circumstances that led to my adoption and I want her to know how happy my life was with my adopted parents."

"Grandma gave you up for adoption?" Rachel asked, stepping closer, letting her presence be known at last.

Jenny's heart sank to the pit of her stomach when she glanced up to find Rachel standing only a few feet away, her blue eyes so wide with bewilderment they looked as if they might pop right out of her head. Jenny looked again at Rick to see if he planned to answer that question or if he would rather she did.

"How long have you been standing there?" Rick wanted to know, his eyebrows pulled low while he quickly tried to decide what he should tell her.

"Long enough to hear what you said about Jenny being adopted and about how the real reason she came here was so she could meet Grandma." Not wanting to give them the opportunity to figure a way out of telling her the truth, she quickly sat in one of the empty chairs near her father and crossed her arms. "So what's the story?"

Rick considered refusing to tell Rachel anything more than she had already overheard, but decided she had a right to know. By the time he had filled her in on what had happened and why Jenny was there Rachel was leaning forward, bubbling with excitement. Rather than seeming in any way disturbed by her grandmother's long-kept "secret," she appeared thoroughly intrigued by it all.

When she finally opened her mouth to make her first remark, it was not to ask how such a thing could have happened or why it had been kept such a deep, dark secret for so long. The first comment out of her mouth came in the form of a simple question directed at Jenny. "So are you my aunt or what?"

Relieved by his daughter's nonjudgmental attitude, Rick smiled and cocked his right eyebrow before answering. "In this case, she's definitely an *or what*."

Rachel laughed and leaned back in her chair to look at Jenny in this new light. "Too bad you were adopted, Dad." She did not wait to be asked why before supplying an explanation. "If you had been Grandma's real son, then Jenny would be your half sister, wouldn't she?"

Rick looked at Jenny triumphantly. "But as it is, she's no real kin to me at all, is she?"

"No, and I guess she's no real kin to me either, huh?" She pulled her pretty features into a puzzled frown. "That's too bad. I'd love to have her for my aunt."

"Just be glad you have her for a friend," Rick said, gazing at Jenny appreciatively. "I know I am."

Jenny felt a strong undercurrent in his voice and shivered, aware the conversation he had wanted to have earlier now lay just a few hours ahead—that conversation he'd claimed would be *about us*.

Chapter Twelve

That evening during supper Rachel was the happiest she had been since Jenny's arrival. She laughed at her father's flimsiest jokes, which only encouraged him to tell more, and even told a few of her own—something she had rarely done.

Whenever Rick made a comment that sounded even the least bit "fatherly," she didn't lash out at him as she would have in the past. In several cases she actually agreed with him. It was as if a silent understanding had been reached between father and daughter, touching Jenny's heart in a way it hadn't been touched in years.

By eight-thirty, when time came for Rachel to go upstairs to get ready to go to the hospital, she and her father were on such good terms she felt brave enough to offer her own opinion about how they should handle Jenny's situation.

"If it was up to me," she said as she stood to go upstairs to wash her hands and brush her hair, "I think I'd probably tell that doctor to hurry up and find some way to make Grandma well enough so Jenny could meet her. After all, Jenny only has about two weeks left. I'm sure she'd prefer to spend at least part of those last two weeks getting to know Grandma.''

"I'm sure she would," Rick agreed, glancing at Jenny uncomfortably. "And Dr. Weathers is doing all he can to help your grandmother get well enough so Jenny can finally meet her. You know that."

"Still, there must be some way to hurry this thing along," Rachel commented, her pretty dark blond eyebrows drawn into a concerned frown. "What if the next two weeks go by and Jenny still hasn't gotten to meet Grandma? It just doesn't seem fair that she's come all this way and hasn't even got to meet her."

"No, it doesn't seem very fair," he acknowledged. "But if there was some way to hurry this thing along, Dr. Weathers or I would have already thought of it. It takes time for emotional wounds to heal. I'm afraid we have no other choice but to allow nature to take its own course and in its own time."

"Still, it doesn't seem fair."

Rick studied Rachel's concerned expression for several seconds. "Don't you take it upon yourself to tell Grandma about any of this, thinking that might force us to allow them to meet. It is important that we wait for Dr. Weathers's approval."

"I won't," Rachel promised, her frown deepening. "But I still hope Grandma gets well in a hurry." Her eyes then glittered and her frown lifted into a speculative smile. "I can hardly wait to hear what she has to say when she finds out Jenny is here."

IT WAS NINE-THIRTY before Rick and Rachel returned from the hospital, and as had become her custom Jenny met them at the back door, eager to hear the latest report on her mother's health.

"She's sitting up a lot better. In fact, she had the back of her bed cranked up until it almost looked like some sort of oversized chair. And when Grandpa got mentioned, she didn't cry nearly as much as she used to," Rachel said, hoping to encourage Jenny. "I think that alone was probably a good sign."

"But not quite good enough," Rick put in quickly, not wanting Jenny to get her hopes up only to have them dashed yet again. "I talked to Dr. Weathers before we left the hospital and he still doesn't think she's ready to have Jenny dropped on her."

"You make me sound like a bomb," Jenny complained good-naturedly, although in a way she knew it was an appropriate comparison.

Rachel laughed at the visual image that came to mind. "You'd sure make a big mess if you were. Why, there'd be parts of you everywhere."

Rick laughed, too, preferring to keep the mood light. "I guess it would be to our advantage to make sure she never explodes. It would take weeks to clean up such a mess."

"Probably would be easier just to move," Rachel agreed. Her blue eyes sparkled with amusement, while she watched the rankled expression on Jenny's face grow deeper.

Tapping her fingertips together, Jenny looked at her with a speculative eyebrow arched with warning. "Just for that, I won't share any of the popcorn I made while you two were gone."

"Popcorn?" Rachel asked, her eyes suddenly round with anticipation. "You made popcorn?"

"Sure did. Since Jacqueline had already gone off to bed by the time I realized I wanted any, I went on into the kitchen and popped it myself."

"Where is it?"

"In a big bowl on the coffee table in the den," Jenny told her.

Eager to taste it, Rachel hurried off down the hall, leaving Rick and Jenny behind.

"I'll go get the lemonade I made to go with it," she said, turning away from Rick, eager not to be alone with him, which was the whole reason she had made popcorn in the first place. She did not want Rachel running off to her room to watch television by herself until she fell asleep, which was slowly becoming her habit. Jenny knew from prior experience, once Rachel had gone upstairs for the night, they would not see her again until morning. Rick would surely realize the opportunity and start in on that conversation he warned her about that morning.

"I doubt it works," Rick called out to Jenny, watching her with perceptively lowered lashes when she turned around to glance at him.

"You doubt what works?"

"The popcorn. If I know Rachel, she'll end up getting her own bowl, filling it with popcorn and still going on up to her room. She knows I am planning to watch the news at ten and she hates watching the news."

Jenny's eyebrows dipped low and her mouth fell into a thin line while she wondered if she had one of those flashing readout signs on the back of her head informing Rick exactly what was on her mind. Rather than deny the truth, she simply shrugged and hurried on toward the kitchen.

Exactly as Rick had predicted, Rachel entered the kitchen scarcely a minute later to find her own bowl. By the time Jenny had the pitcher of lemonade out of the refrigerator and onto a tray with a small bowl of ice and three tall glasses, Rachel had already snatched a Diet Coke out of the bottom drawer and was on her way back to the den to abscond with a sizable portion of the popcorn.

When Jenny entered the room just seconds after Rachel had left, Rick sat on the sofa watching her with a wide, satisfied "I-told-you-so" grin stretched across his handsome face.

Jenny's heart raced with mounting apprehension and her mouth leveled into a flat line, when she noticed that not only was Rachel already gone but someone had gone to the trouble to turn out two of the three lamps in the room.

"Don't tell me," she muttered while she cautiously moved closer to him, quietly setting the tray on the table in front of the sofa. "Rachel has already scooped up her share of the popcorn and left for her room."

"Does appear that way," he said and indicated the now half-empty glass bowl sitting on the coffee table. "One thing you'll learn about Rachel, she loves popcorn. That's why I told her to be sure and take as much as she thought she could possibly eat. I didn't want to risk her returning downstairs for more and overhearing yet another of our private conversations."

He then patted the sofa cushion beside him with the flat of his hand. "Come sit down. I think it is time we have that talk."

"About what?" Jenny asked, trying to pretend she had no idea what he meant. While she swallowed back her mounting apprehension, her gaze wandered involuntarily over the fascinating smile that remained stretched across his face, causing those adorable dimples to sink well into his cheeks. How she would love to trace those dimples with the tips of her fingers.

"About us," he answered honestly. Again, he glanced down and patted the section of sofa beside him. Having sat in the very center of the sofa that would normally seat no more than four, he had reduced the space left for her into a disarmingly small section.

When his blue gaze rose to meet hers again, his expression became so intense, so determined, Jenny felt an unmistakable current pass between them. It made her immediately aware of the very real danger that awaited her, should she sit as close as he wanted.

"What about us?" she asked, wondering if he would become very angry with her if she chose to sit somewhere else.

"First you sit," he summoned in a deep, masculine voice. "Then we talk." When she again glanced at the sofa indecisively, he added, "Right here beside me so we are less likely to be overheard. What I have to say is rather personal."

"Why don't I just close the hall door instead?" she suggested hopefully.

"That's a good idea. Why don't you do both?" he said, his eyebrows lifting at the thought. "But don't just close the door, lock it, then come sit here beside me."

Rather than risk making him angry at a time she really did not want him angry with her, Jenny did what he had asked. First she gently closed the door, then twisted the lock into place before returning to sit beside him on the sofa.

Aware of how precariously close they sat, she inched back against the multicolored throw pillows tilted against the padded arm of the sofa, then turned her body to face him at an abrupt angle. She was careful to sit with her feet tucked under her and her knees protruding between them, thinking that should help keep a safe distance between them while they discussed whatever it was Rick was so determined to discuss.

Rick chuckled. "When I was a teenager I was told that a boy could tell if a girl was truly interested in him by how she positioned herself when she sat beside him," he commented, his blue eyes twinkling with amusement. "I was told that if she was indeed interested in me she would sit with her knees pointed slightly toward me, and if she wasn't interested she'd sit with her knees pointed straight ahead or even pointed away from me."

He paused for the comment to sink in, then glanced down at her cotton-clad knees and added, with a grin, "Well, if that is the case, then you must be far more interested in me than you've let on because your knees are practically buried in my side."

Jenny blushed, but refused to comment about something so absurd. "What is it you wanted to talk about?"

"I told you," he answered, resting his arm along the back of the sofa, his hand mere inches away from her shoulder. "I want to talk about us. I think it is time we were clear on something."

"Oh? And what's that?" she asked, her insides spinning crazily when she realized his hand lay close enough that if he as much as flexed his fingers he would touch her.

"Well, for one thing, I want it made clear once and for all that I am not, never was, and never will be your brother—biological or otherwise. Even Rachel was perceptive enough to realize we are not really related. Why can't you?''

When Jenny opened her mouth to try to explain her feelings one last time, her words were cut short by a deep, meaningful warning from Rick.

"And don't try using that lame excuse that we share the same mother. You know as well as I do that doesn't make us brother and sister. It just means we have something rather unique in common. And as you probably can recall there are several *other* things we have in common, too. One in particular comes readily to mind.'' His eyes glittered with the tantalizing memories of the kiss they'd shared in the darkened garage just a few nights ago.

"Oh?'' was all Jenny could think to say, having had her best argument taken away from her before she could even speak it aloud. Her heart pounded vigorously when she remembered how a similar conversation about other things they had in common had ended. Tiny jolts of excitement shot through her at the vivid memory his words had evoked, still able to feel his strong arms around her and his mouth working passionately to bring her the utmost pleasure.

"Jenny, I can't let you continue using such a poor excuse to keep us apart. It is time that you faced the truth. There is something very special between us, something far too special to be ignored any longer. I know I felt it the very first moment I set eyes on you, before you ever bothered to tell me who you were.''

Jenny could not deny her feelings, but that still did not make it right, nor did it make it safe. It was then she realized that she was more afraid of the relationship than anything else, afraid of being hurt again.

"But what will your friends say?" she tried to reason with him, still clinging to the only excuse she knew that might keep them apart.

"That I'm pretty darned lucky to have found someone like you," he stated frankly.

"Not after they discover the unusual circumstances that brought us together." She still wanted him to see how it might look to others.

Rick bent his head forward to emphasize his words. "It doesn't matter what circumstances brought us together. What matters is that we indeed have been brought together. Why can't you see that our being together was somehow meant to be? Why can't you let down this invisible barrier you've thrown up between us and see what happens?"

"Because," she started to answer but for the life of her could not finish the sentence, still startled to have finally realized the truth—*Because I'm afraid of being hurt again. Because I'm afraid you'll only want me for now, but after a while you'll grow tired of me and you'll toss me aside like yesterday's mail. Because I'm terrified of being rejected again.*

"Because *why?*" he encouraged, able to see that painful thoughts were running rampant through her mind and wanting to know just what they were. He leaned forward, slipping his arm farther along the top of the sofa behind her until it lightly touched her neck.

Aware he fully intended to kiss her again, Jenny's heartbeat quickened, sending a frenzied tingle of excitement through her bloodstream, and her body tensed, frozen with an opposing combination of fear and desire. Although she still was not all that sure it was the right thing to do, she did nothing to prevent the kiss. When his free hand gently pushed her knees downward to move them out of the way, she willingly obliged.

"Jenny, I don't think I've ever wanted a woman as much as I want you right now," he said, his voice but a tender whisper that fell softly against her cheek while his mouth continued to move ever closer to hers.

Jenny's heart soared, aware by the deep timbre of his voice the words he'd just spoken had been the truth. How good it felt to know that someone like Rick actually wanted her. After having lived with so many traumatic rejections in her life, being "wanted" was exactly what she longed for—although she had not really realized it before now. If only she didn't have to worry about what would happen when he didn't want her anymore—which was a possibility she had to consider, if for no other reason than self-preservation.

"Jenny, tell me you want me as much as I want you," he said, his lips so close to hers she felt the warm vibration of his voice.

"I do," she admitted in a choked voice, her fear of being hurt battling her sudden desire to be held. "I do want you. I want you very much, but—"

"No buts," he cautioned. His eyelids lowered heavily over his glimmering blue eyes. "Not now. Not *ever*. Either you want me or you don't."

Rather than offer further comment, Jenny decided to take the chance of being hurt again and lifted her arms to accept his coming embrace. She tilted her head back just before their parted lips met in wondrous accord, sending sudden shock waves of pleasure through them both.

Jenny knew that although she still feared being hurt again, she would not turn away. Not this time. When she pulled her mouth free of his, it was to take a much-needed breath, not to try to push him away.

"Jenny, I think I very well may have fallen in love with you," he said, taking advantage of the few seconds their lips were parted to speak what was on his mind. "No, I take that back, I *know* I have fallen in love with you. I have no doubts whatever. I only hope that some day you will put aside your foolish notions about what people will think and grow to love me, too."

Jenny was too shocked by this sudden declaration of love to think clearly enough to explain that she had already fallen in love with him. That was her main problem. If she hadn't fallen in love with him she would never have let him kiss her like that, nor would she have allowed him to hold her so intimately close. But at the moment all her befuddled brain would allow her to do in response to his words was moan appreciatively while his mouth descended on hers yet again.

Instantly Rick's arms tightened around her, drawing her closer. Jenny responded by returning the powerful embrace, pressing her body as close as possible while still remaining upright on the sofa. When his tongue dipped lightly into her mouth, teasing the sensitive inner lining of her lips, she returned the favor in kind, savoring the tantalizing taste that was uniquely Rick.

The gentle fragrance of his after-shave mixed with her sweet floral scent to create a heady, intoxicating aroma of sensuality, making her that much more aware of him.

With her barriers temporarily brought down and her heart open to further exploration, Jenny eagerly crushed her body against his while he continued to cast his wondrous magic over her. When he broke his mouth free from hers to ravish gentle kisses on her silken brown hair, she closed her eyes to enjoy the feel of the light, titillating pressure against the top of her head.

While his lips slowly worked their way downward across her forehead, then on toward her still-parted lips, her hands roamed freely over the smooth surface of his pale blue knit pullover shirt until she could stand it no longer. She had to know what it felt like to touch his skin.

Eagerly she slid her hands down past his waist, to where the banded hem of his shirt had risen above his waistband in the back. Finding such a convenient opening, she plunged both hands beneath the soft fabric. She felt so extremely exhilarated when her fingertips finally touched the firm muscles of his lower back that her toes curled in response.

At first she was satisfied to simply explore the area she had exposed along his lower back by pushing the shirt up, but the muscles across his upper back and shoulders quickly beckoned. She plunged her hands higher still, until she had explored all those areas to the fullest, then moved on to run her fingertips lightly over the crisp texture of the body hairs patterned across his chest.

The warmth from his skin intensified the already sensitive tips of her fingertips when she next felt the flat plane of his stomach and stopped to explore the hollow of his navel.

A deep, sensual sound welled deep in Rick's throat while he leaned over to turn out the only light brightening the area. When he returned to her the room held only the faint glow of moonlight that filtered in soft, shimmering waves through the nearby windows.

Still wanting her as he'd wanted no other, Rick's hands went immediately to the front of Jenny's blouse where he quickly worked with the tiny buttons that held it together while he kissed her hungrily.

Seconds later his mouth again broke away from hers and sent tiny electric shivers through her body when he then bent to kiss the sensitive areas just below her ear and moved slowly downward along her neck—all the while continuing his work with her buttons. They were both consumed by the sheer passion that had provoked such frantic needs.

Jenny felt the cool rush of air over her skin when he finally parted the upper portion of her blouse. She next felt the backs of his fingers brush lightly against her skin while he hurried to complete the lower buttons. Once he finally finished his task, he gripped the edges of the material with his fingers and slipped the garment back from her shoulders, gently tugging until it had come off entirely. She responded first by tugging off her shoes with her toes, then by gently pulling his shirt up over his head.

She waited until he had removed the tiny scrap that was her bra and had tossed it aside before reaching out for him again. They were now both bare to the waist, the silvery light from the windows falling across their skin with a gentle glow. Their passion spiraled ever higher as once again their lips found each other.

Pressing against him, she felt the marvel of his firm, fit body against her soft, supple breasts. The crisp texture of his body hair tickled the delicate peaks when she moved against him.

Her slow, sensual movement aroused him further, for he quickly stood, pulling her up with him, and began to work frantically with the large buttons that held the front of her cotton jeans. Within seconds, he had the soft blue material pushed down over her hips and after a few extra tugs had them completely off her and tossed carelessly on the floor. Except for her lacy panties, she stood nude before him, her body literally glowing in the muted moonlight.

"You are every bit as beautiful as I thought you'd be," he said, glancing down at her for a moment before bending to kiss her neck lightly.

Jenny closed her eyes against the delicious shiver that resulted from the tantalizing feel of his lips and tongue against her skin. She was only vaguely aware that while his mouth continued to trail feathery kisses down her neck and across her collarbone he had begun removing the rest of his own clothing. She would have gladly assisted, but within only a few seconds he was even more naked than she.

Bending again, he removed her final garment and paused to admire her beauty a second time before he gently pulled her back down upon the sofa. When they embraced again, they were able to enjoy the feel of each other's bodies to the fullest. While Rick's lips returned to make gentle yet persistent contact with hers, she delighted in the feel of his body naked against hers. Her hands roamed eagerly over the now unencumbered muscles along his back and strained to feel the taut muscles along the sides of his hips and upper thighs. The lightly haired skin felt good to her touch, arousing her more.

While she continued her gentle exploration, Rick's hands moved to do a bit of exploring themselves. He first caressed her supple shoulders with the inner curves of his fingers, then ran a smooth course down her sides with the flats of his palms, causing her skin to come alive with eager anticipation.

Slowly he pulled his mouth free of hers yet again. He took several deep, needed breaths while he moved downward, allowing his mouth to caress the straining peak of one breast. His tongue teased the hardened tip with short, tantalizing strokes, causing her to arch her back impatiently. He then moved to the neglected breast and quickly brought it an equal share of ecstasy.

Exhilarated to the point of madness, Jenny was not certain how much longer she could bear the bittersweet onslaught, nor was she sure how to coax him to stop this magnificent torture and bring her the relief she sought. She pulled gently at his shoulder, but his mouth continued to bring her breast unbearable waves of unadulterated pleasure. She writhed from the delectable sensations building inside her, and from the persistent ache that had grown to a painful intensity and had centered itself somewhere deep in her abdomen. Her body craved relief from that which it had so long been denied. She moaned aloud, making him audibly aware of her need.

Drawing on first one breast, then the other one last time, Rick moved to fulfill her, quickly bringing their passion to an ultimate height. When release came for Jenny, only moments before it came for Rick, it was so wondrous and shattering she had to bite her lower lip to keep from crying aloud with pleasure.

With Rick still lying more atop her than beside her, they sank slowly into the supreme depths of satisfaction and for the moment Jenny refused to worry about anything. She merely enjoyed the warmth of his body next to hers and knew at least for now Rick wanted her.

JENNY CONTINUED NOT TO worry about where her budding relationship with Rick might eventually lead, or even to try to figure out exactly where she would like for it to go. That night, after she had gone to bed, the only thought to enter her mind before she drifted off into a sweet, peaceful sleep, was the very real fact that she loved Rick and because she did love him so deeply she just might find some way to fit into his and Rachel's lives after all. She might never be allowed to become a permanent part of what those two shared, but she was willing to accept that fact. She was happy enough to be participating in their lives at all—at least for now.

The next morning when she awoke, she felt the warm feeling of acceptance still filling her heart. She and Rick might not have made any everlasting commitments to each other the previous night, but they had both accepted the fact that something very special had developed between them. They had both admitted they cared deeply for each other and they both believed those feelings were the sort that would not go away easily. Although there was no way to know how such a relationship would end, or even if it would end, they were both willing to give it a chance.

Other than the decision to give it a try, there had been no verbal commitments made between them, but then it was really too soon for that. First they needed to explore the strong feelings they had developed for one another and see just how lasting they were. If they then found the bonds to be strong enough, and the desire dominating enough, they could discuss real commitment.

For now, Jenny was content just knowing Rick wanted to try. When she climbed out of bed that next day, she felt more rested than she had since her arrival. Within minutes she had showered, dressed, put on her makeup and headed downstairs to see if Rick seemed as happy as she about what had transpired between them.

When she opened the bedroom door to step out into the hallway, she let out a startled scream. She had not expected to find him standing only a few feet away, his hand raised in midair, as if prepared to knock. When she noticed the serious expression on his face, she became even more alarmed. He looked as if he was already having second thoughts about what had happened last night.

"You scared me half to death," she said, her hand pressed protectively against her breastbone.

When he then grinned that disarming off-center grin of his, she realized that what he had come to her room to say was not quite as serious as she had first feared.

"Sorry about that, but I wanted to talk with you before you went down to breakfast."

Again curious about why he'd come to her room, her brows drew together. She stepped back to let him enter. "What about?"

"About Mother."

Jenny's heart flew to ~~her throat~~. "What about her? Is she worse?"

"No, nothing like that. It's just that I did some serious thinking about your problem last night."

"My problem?" Jenny asked, still wondering where this conversation would lead.

"Yes," he nodded then motioned for her to sit down. He waited until she had done so before explaining, "I spent most of last night trying to figure out some way for you to meet Mother before you have to leave." Although he did not like the idea of her returning to West Texas in what was now less than two weeks, he knew it was inevitable, and he thought she deserved to meet her biological mother at least once before she went. "I think I have finally come up with a solution."

"A solution?"

"Yes, and what I've come up with is really quite simple."

Jenny shook her head, not yet fully understanding. "Wait a minute, a solution to what?"

"To your problem," he reiterated, frowning that she had yet to grasp what he meant. "You have less than two weeks left before you have to return to work, and you have yet to meet Mother."

Jenny's eyes widened with hope. "And?"

"And I thought you might like to go with me to the hospital this afternoon to meet her."

"But what about Dr. Weathers? He told you just last night that she was not ready to be told about me."

"I don't plan to tell **her** *about* you. I simply plan to introduce her *to* you—as a friend of mine. Which is not entirely misleading," he added with a devilish smile, "because after last night, I'd say we have become *very* close friends."

Jenny couldn't help but return his playful smile, so overcome by the different emotions trying to win her attention she thought she might burst with excitement. "Yes, I'd say so, too."

"Of course, I will want to discuss this idea with Dr. Weathers to make sure he agrees that no harm could come of it," Rick went on to say. "But if he has no objections, and I don't think he will, you can expect me to be by for you around one-thirty. Now that she's in her own room, she is governed by the regular visiting hours. Although I can go in whenever I want, non-family members are restricted to those regular visiting hours and as far as everyone else is concerned, you are still a non-family member." He paused. Then when all she did was stare at him with continued open-eyed amazement, he grinned and asked, "Is that all right with you?"

"All right?" she repeated, bursting with enthusiasm. "It's about as all right as anything can possibly get. I can hardly wait." She then gave her closet a worried glance. "I wonder what I should wear."

"Wear what you have on," he said, finding nothing wrong with the white shorts and blouse she wore. "If you came in too dressed up during the middle of the week, Mother might think you odd."

"It's just that I want to make a very good first impression."

"You will," he assured her, his smile deepening. "You can't do anything but."

"Oh, you silver-tongued devil," she teased, thickening her already deep southern accent. "How those honeyed words do slip off your tongue."

"I speak only the truth," he said, looking down at her appreciatively while he bent forward to kiss her. "Just see that you are ready at one-thirty."

Chapter Thirteen

Jenny's heart pounded with such torrential force that when she and Rick stepped off the elevator and onto the hospital's third floor, she was not sure she would be able to bear the onslaught much longer. Thinking of what lay just ahead, she moistened her lips by running the tip of her tongue between them and tried her very best to keep her breathing at a normal rate.

"How far?" she asked, staring ahead at the many doors evenly spaced on either side of the wide, gleaming corridor. Tiny bumps of apprehension formed beneath her skin while she followed just a few steps behind Rick.

"Near the end of the hall," he answered. When he glanced back and noticed how pale she looked, he reached out a supportive arm to her. "Don't be so afraid. She will love you."

"That is, until she finds out who I really am," Jenny muttered, then curled her hands into tight fists as if that might help control her floundering heartbeat in some way. The muscles in her body had pulled so tight with her mounting apprehension, it made it hard for her to walk. Her mouth felt as if it had been lined with cotton. "I can just imagine what she's going to think when she eventually learns who I am."

"She'll love you even then—especially then," he assured her, giving her shoulders a gentle squeeze while drawing her into the crook of his arm.

A slow, tingling warmth spread through her shoulders with a spilling, languid ease. How she wished she could relax and enjoy the tantalizing feeling, but there was no time for that. She was finally about to fulfill her quest.

Rick dipped forward and pressed a gentle, reassuring kiss to her temple, causing a flood tide of vibrant sensations to cascade through her. She was deeply touched by his apparent efforts to ease her trepidation.

"Mother can't help but love you," he continued, his voice so deep and so rich with emotion it sent another wave of relaxing warmth through Jenny. "No one can help but love someone like you."

"Robert managed not to," she quipped, not really knowing why she said it other than it was a viable argument.

"Robert was a fool," he stated bluntly then paused in the hallway to look at her directly. His eyes glittered with several different emotions while he studied her still-worried expression. "Jenny, if you go in there looking like that, Mother is going to know something peculiar is going on and she's the type to want to know what it is. She'll ask questions you might not be ready to answer yet."

Gently he massaged the bunched muscles at her shoulders and bent his head forward until his forehead pressed against hers. "Try to keep in mind you are not headed into the lion's den. Just calm down. Relax. Be yourself.''

"Easy for you to say," she muttered, letting out a quick, exasperated breath. "You've already met the woman." Her foot started to tap anxiously against the gleaming tile from having stood still too long. The energy inside her had been building all day until it was bursting to find an outlet.

Rick chuckled at her unexpected remark. "Yes, I've met her and she's really a nice person. You'll see. Now take several deep breaths and count to ten.''

He waited until she had done as told before slipping his arm around her shoulders and directing her toward the nearest door. "Let's go. This is her room."

Jenny's heart jumped immediately to her throat. The hour of reckoning had arrived. She was now only a few seconds away from meeting the woman who had chosen to give her life. Although in a way she dreaded this initial encounter, afraid she would do or say something wrong, at the same time she could hardly wait to see what her biological mother was like.

With her eyes trained on the closed door, Jenny's excitement slowly overcame her fear, though not completely. She eagerly anticipated the sound of her birth mother's voice, the first glimpse of her smile, eager to see her many facial expressions, but most of all, she was anxious to hear her laugh.

For some reason, it was extremely important to Jenny that before they left the hospital she hear her birth mother's laughter.

Filled with a frightful case of the jitters, Jenny crossed her arms over her stomach and prepared for the worst, yet hoped for the best.

Rick knocked lightly on the door, then gently pushed it open, drawing Jenny inside with him. He still held his arm around her, as much to offer his strength as his support when they stepped into the room.

Jenny felt his arm give her one last quick squeeze as if to tell her to keep her courage when the only occupant of the room glanced up from her magazine and discovered she had two visitors instead of one. Immediately Jenny's eyes widened. She quickly drank in every little detail about her, aware of how different she looked today than she had weeks earlier. When awake, her birth mother's face was full of vigor and life, her expression filled with animation.

"Hi, Mother," Rick said, sounding as if nothing was out of the ordinary. With his arm still supporting Jenny, he slowed her to a halt just a few feet away from where their mother lay in a raised hospital bed, reading. "How are you feeling?"

"Now that they have finally plucked the last of those ridiculous tubes out of my arms and are feeding me halfway decent meals, I'm feeling much better," she responded, though with no animosity. She then looked at Jenny with a questioning lift of her eyebrow, dividing her attention between Jenny's pensive expression and the fact that Rick had his arm around her. "Fact is, I'm about ready to break out of this place." Her mouth flattened into a playful yet menacing scowl. "But Doc says it will be weeks yet before I am allowed to go home."

Jenny trembled imperceptibly, her eyes burning with unshed tears from the mere sound of her own mother's voice. It was a voice very much like her own, sort of deep and mellow—and definitely Texan.

My own mother's voice, her mind repeated in wonder, her heart pounding so rapidly she could feel it rushing the blood through all parts of her body. How exhilarating it was to know she was finally face-to-face with the very woman who had given her life.

"Well, son?" Elizabeth asked, setting the magazine on her bedside table and crossing her arms impatiently. "Are you going to introduce me or not?"

"I think not," Rick teased, then brought Jenny closer. Without releasing her entirely, he bent to offer his mother a light kiss on the cheek. "You have a tendency to ask too many questions whenever I introduce you to any of my friends."

"I do not," she protested, then looked at Jenny directly, as if appraising her from this closer vantage point and liking what she saw.

Jenny felt an odd, shivering warmth spread over her when Elizabeth Anderson then smiled, because it was a deep, all-consuming smile that radiated outward to touch everyone and everything in the room. She was glad to discover her birth mother was every bit as nice and as good-natured as she had hoped. But, then, judging by what Rick and Rachel had told her, she'd expected as much.

"Since my son had chosen to be so *rude,* I guess I'll just have to ask you myself," Elizabeth said with an affable shrug, undaunted by Rick's teasing comments. "Who are you?"

"See there?" Rick said, raising a finger in triumph, eager to prove his point. He leaned toward his mother, his blue eyes narrowed as if to say I-told-you-so. "She hasn't been in here a full minute and you are already asking her questions. You can't keep from it, can you?"

Elizabeth arched an eyebrow as if offering a silent but playful warning. "You left me little choice. You know how insatiable my curiosity can be."

Rick laughed and looked at Jenny with a pleased smile. "Then I guess I'd better toss that ravenous curiosity of yours a morsel or two to appease its appetite. This is Jenny Ryan. She's a very good friend of mine." He put special emphasis on the word friend, hoping to spare Jenny his mother's bold attempts at matchmaking.

"If she's such a very good friend, why is it I have never met her?"

"Because she's a *new* very good friend of mine," he stressed. "And because I wanted her to get to know me a little better before I let you have a shot at her."

"Oh? Then she's a *special* new very good friend?" Elizabeth said, and smiled approvingly while again she let her gaze roam over Jenny's pretty face and her stylish shorts outfit.

"Yes, I think you could say she's a very special new very good friend of mine," he agreed with a slight chuckle when he realized how ludicrous that sounded. Then to prove how special Jenny was to him, he tightened his arm around her shoulders to draw her closer against him, as much in a show of affection as to help her stay on her feet. Her shoulders had been trembling slightly since they first entered.

"Well, it's about time," Elizabeth told him, then held her hand out to Jenny. Her dark brown eyes sparkled with approval.

Aware she was about to touch the very woman who had given her life, Jenny's breath lodged in her throat. She swallowed hard to clear it, then slowly held her hands out to her. She felt an overwhelming sense of belonging when the woman took those trembling hands in her own and held them firmly.

"What on earth are you so afraid of?" Elizabeth asked with a peculiar expression, having felt the tremors in Jenny's hands, then looked accusingly at Rick. "What has he told you about me?"

"There you go with *more* of your never-ending questions," Rick pointed out before he cocked his head to one side, his expression one of feigned innocence. "All I told her was that your bark was considerably worse than your bite. And that if you did happen to draw blood, we'd be right here in the hospital where she could get immediate and proper care."

"How kind of you to be so reassuring," Elizabeth said, then again looked at Jenny. "Please don't take anything my son says seriously. He has such a wild imagination." She then glanced back at Rick, her eyebrow again arched, but this time with a mother's pride. "But basically he's a good boy."

"Boy?" Rick protested as if injured by her choice of words. "I happen to be thirty-two years old now." With Jenny no longer in the circle of his arm, he tossed his hands up to reveal his indignation. "Don't I run the family business—*alone?* Aren't I the father of a thirteen-year-old girl, and wasn't I also a husband for well over a decade? Tell me, when do I ever reach the status of being a fully grown man?"

"There you go," Elizabeth shot back, narrowing her dark brown eyes perceptively while she slowly shook her head. "Asking a lot of your never-ending questions." She then turned to Jenny, her eyes again sparkling with amusement. "That son of mine is always asking questions. He never stops."

"Touché," Rick said begrudgingly, then his eyes lit with a fitting idea. Crossing his arms over his chest, he looked at her with a triumphant expression. "Tell you what, Mother, I won't ask any more questions, if you won't."

"But then how will I ever find out how you two met? How will I ever know what she does for a living?"

"There you go asking more questions."

When Elizabeth laughed, it fell golden and sweet against Jenny's ear. "Well, then, can I at least comment on how beautiful this stranger is, whom you have brought into my room without bothering to do much more than offer me her name?"

"That was still a question," he pointed out.

"But it also bears the truth. I don't know where you found her—and since I'm obviously not allowed to ask any more questions, I will probably never know how you two came to meet—but whoever she is, she's quite a looker."

"That's true," he agreed willingly, and stepped forward to put his arm around Jenny again. "But that's because she looks so much like her mother, who also happens to be very attractive. I suppose you could say good looks run in the family."

Jenny glanced back at him and grinned. "I'll have to agree with that."

Elizabeth looked at them with a peculiar expression. "How fortunate for you both to be so beautiful. Maybe I will be allowed to meet your mother someday. Are you and your family from around here?"

"Mo-ther," Rick sang, as if to point out that had been yet another question.

"All right," she conceded with a flattening of her mouth, a mouth very much like Jenny's. "I'll admit it. I'm a nosy person. I always have been and I always will be. Now will you just tell me if she's from around here or whether you imported her from somewhere else?"

"I'm imported," Jenny supplied, seeing no harm in answering some less personal questions about herself. "I'm from West Texas. I'm only in Tyler for a few more weeks—visiting friends."

Elizabeth frowned, disappointed. "That's too bad. I had hoped—" She paused to decide how to word it without raising Rick's immediate ire.

"You'd hoped to play matchmaker," Rick put in for her, then explained to Jenny, "Ever since my divorce became final, she's been after me to start dating."

"Well, it's about time you did," Elizabeth said, her tone suddenly serious. "I worry about you, son. All work and no play is not healthy. Look what it did to your father."

"But Dad wasn't all work and no play," Rick reminded her. "He loved to play. He loved to go on trips and take the entire family with him."

Elizabeth smiled fondly, her eyes misting with the tender memories he'd invoked. "That he did. He knew how to enjoy life." She then blinked several times before she could shake the sad feeling. "But that is beside the point."

"And what point is that?"

"That you need a woman in your life," she stated bluntly. "Someone like this beautiful young woman here."

Jenny felt a little taken aback by Elizabeth's bold nature, but grinned at her tenacity. The woman did not give up easily, which was obviously a trait she had installed into Rick, probably at a very early age.

"Too bad she lives so far away," Elizabeth continued, her attractive face drawn into a disappointed frown. "I like the way she looks at you."

Jenny's eyes flew open at such a remark. She hadn't realized she had looked at him at all. "How do I look at him?"

"Like a woman in love is supposed to look at a man," Elizabeth said with her usual frankness. "That's why I wish you lived closer." She then grinned again and arched a speculative eyebrow. "Any chance of convincing you to move to Tyler?"

Although Rick might normally have fielded that question for Jenny, he was curious to hear the answer himself, so he, too, waited for her response.

"I'm afraid I have both a good job and a nice house waiting for me in Stockfield."

"No boyfriend?" Elizabeth wanted to know.

"No, no boyfriend."

"Any children?"

"No, no children. Just a mindless mutt named Walter."

Elizabeth's forehead knotted while she considered this new bit of information. "But you said you have friends here in Tyler. Maybe they will help convince you to move. Where *are* you staying while you are in Tyler?"

Jenny's eyes widened apprehensively and she looked to Rick to come up with a quick answer, startled when he decided to tell the truth.

"Right now, she's staying at our house. Rachel loves her."

Rather than looking shocked, Elizabeth's face brightened with renewed hope. "Rachel has met her? That scamp. I wonder why she hasn't as much as mentioned her to me?"

"Because I told her not to. I was afraid you'd make more out of Jenny staying with us than was justified."

Elizabeth's expression turned instantly innocent as if to declare his accusations unfounded, but she immediately faced Jenny with more questions. "How much longer are you planning to stay with Rick?"

"Only until a week from Sunday. I have to be back at work on the ninth and it is a full day's drive from here."

"Then that still leaves me ten days," she said with a broad smile, after having done a bit of quick calculation in her head.

"Ten days to do what?" Rick asked, lowering his thick lashes with obvious suspicion.

"Why to convince her to stay in Tyler, of course."

"Mother, you're incorrigible," Rick said, but deep down he knew he planned to do the exact same thing.

Although he knew Jenny was clearly not the type to make such a far-reaching decision without first having given it a lot of thought, he did hope that before time came for her to leave, she would have found a worthwhile reason to stay. And he hoped that worthwhile reason would be him.

After another half hour of friendly chatter between Elizabeth and her son, with Jenny joining in whenever she could, there was another soft knock on the hospital door.

Jenny was disappointed to see three women about Elizabeth's age enter, knowing her time alone with Rick and her mother had come to an abrupt end.

After a few quick introductions, Rick noticed the time and claimed they needed to be on their way. He had a lot of research to do now that he was seriously considering buying that local auto-parts chain.

"Will I see you this evening?" Elizabeth asked, wanting to have a commitment of some sort before he left.

"Don't I always come by every evening?"

"Yes, but I wasn't too sure you'd be coming by this evening, what with your company and all."

Aware all eyes were upon Jenny, he decided not to make her feel any more uncomfortable than she must already be by indicating that *she* was the company his mother had referred to. "I've had company for several weeks now and I've still managed to stop by at least once each evening." He noticed how quickly his mother's eyebrows shot up upon hearing that bit of information. "I'll see you later."

"Be sure to bring Jenny with you when you come. I still have a lot of questions I'd like to ask."

"I don't doubt that," Rick muttered, then guided Jenny out of the room and into the hall. He glanced back over his shoulder toward his mother's room to make certain they were out of earshot. "I really should have warned you about her matchmaking tendencies. She can't stand the thought of me not dating."

"And why don't you date?"

"Because until a few weeks ago, I didn't know anyone I'd care to date." He then bent forward to nuzzle her playfully with his nose while they continued down the hall, making her aware he meant her.

Jenny felt tiny shivers of excitement cascade down her spine, causing little bumps to form beneath the sensitive outer layer of her skin. "But you don't actually date me."

Rick grinned that devil's-own-grin of his. "That's because I don't have to. You already live with me."

Jenny's eyes widened and she glanced around to see if anyone could possibly have overheard such a brash statement.

"I live at your house. I don't actually live with you," she corrected.

"Something I'd love to rectify," he commented, his grin widening at the thought.

Thinking he was just teasing her, Jenny jabbed him lightly in the side. "You are as incorrigible as your mother."

"Watch how you talk about her, she's your mother, too," he pointed out, unaware that would only remind her of the awkwardness of their situation.

"And what a nice mother she is," Jenny said, then fell silent, wondering how long it would be before they could tell Elizabeth the truth. Jenny was more than a friend of Rick's; she was the little baby girl given up for adoption over twenty-nine years ago—all grown up.

BECAUSE ELIZABETH had taken an immediate liking to Jenny she insisted Rick bring her with him every time he and Rachel came to visit. And even though it had yet to come out who Jenny really was, a definite bond started to develop between the two women almost instantly.

It was the Friday before Jenny was scheduled to leave that Dr. Weathers finally decided the time was right to tell Elizabeth the truth.

"I really think she should be told while Jenny is still here," he explained when he'd stopped them in the hall that afternoon. "Tonight when you come to visit, I think Jenny should tell her the truth, the whole truth."

Jenny's eyes widened apprehensively. "Will you be there in case something goes wrong?"

"Of course, I'll be there," Dr. Weathers said. "I want to see Liz's face when you tell her. Therefore I need to know what time you plan to visit tonight."

"We usually come by about seven," Rick said, already pondering the possibilities. "But because that's regular visiting hours, some of her friends might pop in while we are in the middle of telling her. I think it would be better if we came a little early."

"I agree. Let's meet back here at six. I should be through with my rounds by then, and it will also give her plenty of time to recover before her friends start to come by at seven."

It was agreed. That evening they would tell Elizabeth the truth. The afternoon that followed had to be the longest of Jenny's life. Knowing that the truth was finally about to be told, she worried what her birth mother's reaction would be. She had no way to know how she would react. Would she become angry because they had neglected to tell her earlier? Or would she be understanding of the fact that Dr. Weathers had not wanted them to say anything?

By five forty-five, when Jenny climbed into the car with Rick and Rachel, she was a bundle of nerves.

"Will you calm down?" Rick insisted, reaching over to pat her reassuringly on the hand. "You're starting to make *me* nervous."

But Jenny was too worried to calm down. Her heart pumped frantically inside her chest, as if in a futile attempt to wash the panic aside. When they stepped off the elevator at just a few minutes before six and found Dr. Weathers waiting for them halfway down the hall, she wondered if she would have the courage to go through with it.

As had become his custom, Rick wrapped a supportive arm around her shoulders while Rachel took Jenny's right hand in her left. Together they entered the room with Dr. Weathers right behind him.

"What happened?" Elizabeth wanted to know immediately, having noticed how pale Jenny was. She sat forward in bed, trying to determine exactly how serious the problem might be.

"Nothing," Dr. Weathers assured her, stepping around the other three to come to her bedside. When he reached for her hand and felt for her pulse, it was more out of habit than anything else. "It's just that Jenny has something she wants to tell you before she goes back to West Texas. Something we have all agreed you need to hear."

"What is it?" She looked both alarmed and confused while her gaze traveled from one solemn face to another until finally her gaze rested on Jenny. "What do you have to tell me?"

Jenny swallowed back the painful constriction that had tightened around the base of her throat, then stepped forward, away from the others.

"There's something about me that I think you should know."

"What is it?" Elizabeth's eyebrows dipped low with concern. "What should I know?"

Jenny pressed her lips together, then took the deep breath she needed to force the words out of her mouth. "I wanted to tell you when I first arrived, but Dr. Weathers advised against it. He felt you weren't yet well enough to hear it."

"Hear *what?*"

"That I am adopted." She paused to swallow again. "I was born on December 21, 1961 in Denton, Texas, and my name at birth was Katherine Ruth Thornton." She paused for that to soak in before continuing with her planned speech, but before she could state the name of the hospital where she was born or that she had just recently had her adoption records opened, Elizabeth had started to tremble so violently Jenny glanced worriedly back at Rick then looked at Elizabeth again, her expression apologetic.

With tears in her eyes and a voice filled with so much emotion she could hardly continue, she hurried to explain. "I'm not here to cause any trouble. And no one knows who I am or why I've come but the people in this room. I just wanted to meet the woman who gave birth to me."

A long, excruciating silence filled the room while everyone waited to see what Elizabeth's reaction would be. Jenny felt her heart breaking, wishing now she had kept her mouth shut.

Elizabeth continued to tremble all over while she reached for her cover, shoving it impatiently out of the way. Her face had gone deathly pale and her rounded gaze remained fixed on Jenny's face while she slowly slipped out of that bed. When she stood before them in her nightgown, still quivering violently, she was unable to speak. Instead she held her arms out to Jenny and when Jenny went immediately into them, both women wept openly.

It was several long minutes before Jenny pulled away and glanced again at Rick, who was dabbing a suspiciously damp eye with the tip of his third finger. Rachel stood beside him, her arms around his waist, tears spilling freely down her face. Even Dr. Weathers was blinking profusely when he stepped forward to order Elizabeth back into bed.

"Why wouldn't you let her tell me?" Elizabeth demanded to know, looking her friend straight in the eye.

"Because I didn't think you were ready to know."

"Didn't think I was ready?" she repeated incredulously. "You know very well that I've always dreamed of this moment. How can you possibly say you didn't think I was ready?"

"You've been through a lot lately," he reminded her. "I just wanted to be sure you'd recovered from all that before hitting you with this."

Elizabeth looked again at Jenny, her dark eyes filled with wonder. "So, tell me all about you. What were your parents like? Where did you grow up? Do you have any brothers and sisters? Were they adopted, too? Did you always know you were adopted or did you find out after you became an adult?"

Her questions came in such rapid succession, Jenny could not possibly remember them all, but she did her best. "My parents were the most loving, caring people you'd ever want to meet," she reassured her, sitting down on the edge of her bed to make herself more comfortable. "I had a very happy childhood. In fact, because I didn't have any brothers and sisters, I was an only child and I was spoiled rotten. I grew up in—"

While Jenny and Elizabeth became acquainted as mother and daughter, Rick motioned to Rachel and Dr. Weathers that they should leave. Quietly the three slipped out of the room and stood guard over the door, refusing to let anyone else enter until someone had emerged from inside.

But Jenny and Elizabeth hardly noticed they'd gone. They were too caught up in finding out everything there was to know about each other to notice what went on around them.

"I want you to know that it was not my idea to give you up for adoption," Elizabeth said, pressing Jenny's hand against her cheek for the dozenth time. Although she'd had teary spells and dry spells since having discovered Jenny's true identity, she was having another of her teary spells when she went on to explain. "Please understand it was my father's idea. I was sixteen and unmarried when I found out I was pregnant, so I had little choice but to do what my father wanted, which was to give you up for adoption. Had my mother still been alive things might have been different, because she was the sort to find a way around any situation, but she'd been dead for over a year. I only had my father to turn to."

"But what about *my* father?" Jenny asked, ready to know something about him. "What did he have to say about it?"

"He refused to marry me," Elizabeth admitted, looking away from her for the first time since she'd discovered who Jenny really was. "I was a foolish, trusting sixteen-year-old who was conned by an out-of-state college boy out sowing his wild oats, as he so aptly termed it. Yet at the same time he was telling me how much he loved me and how much he needed me, he was already engaged to some girl back home, a girl he refused to give up for any reason.''

"Did he eventually marry that other girl?" Jenny wondered.

"I don't really know. I suppose he did. He certainly didn't want to marry me. But that's why I never told anyone about you. I was so ashamed for having been taken in by that charlatan. The only other person who ever knew about you was my father, and he's the one who arranged for me to come to Texas and have you in secret.''

Elizabeth's voice became more emotionally strained when she continued. "It tore my heart out to have to give you up, but I was barely seventeen when you were born. What could I do?" Her gaze took on a sad, distant quality while she remembered back to that fateful day. "You probably didn't know, but I watched your parents take you away.''

"You did? They let the mothers see the people who were to adopt their children?''

"I didn't say they let me see them. But I saw them all the same.''

"How?''

"I was in the nursery playing with you when Nurse Goodwell came in to shoo me away. Nurse Goodwell's name suited that woman perfectly because she was a tenderhearted thing. That's why I knew something was up when she came into the room and sternly told me to put you down and go do my chores. I tried to explain that I'd already done them, but she insisted I needed to redo them and ordered me on out.''

"Because I knew it was time for them to take you away and because it was so unlike her to behave that way, I knew what was happening. I hurried into Jean's room. In the time we were there, Jean had become a close friend of mine and her room faced the street. Because there was an unfamiliar car out front, I sat at her window and watched until someone finally came outside. It was nearly thirty minutes before I saw a tall, handsome man and a short, pretty young woman leave with you nestled lovingly in the woman's arms. The man was leaning over you, trying to coax you into holding his finger."

Elizabeth closed her eyes, her face contorted with remembered pain. "Although you were too far away to hear me and wouldn't have known what I was saying, had you heard, I called out to you. I told you to behave yourself and to have a good life. I watched until the car drove out of sight, then I turned to Jean and cried for hours."

Jenny was too overcome by emotion to speak right away. It was several seconds before she was able to say what was in her heart. "I know it hurt, but you did the right thing. And although I might not have behaved myself *all* the time, I did have a good life." She sniffed and blinked several times. "I still do for that matter."

Elizabeth stared deeply into Jenny's tear-filled eyes. "I'm so glad you found me. And I'm so glad that you found Rick."

Jenny's forehead twisted with confusion, not really making the connection. "Why is that?"

"Because he needs someone like you. Someone with a good heart, someone who will love him for who and what he is, not for what you want him to become."

"You still feel that way, even though you now know who I really am?"

Elizabeth looked at her as if not understanding what that could possibly have to do with it. "More now than ever. Imagine, two of the people I love most getting together like you have. I just wish you could stay longer than Sunday. There are still so many questions I'd like to ask."

"But I can't keep taking advantage of Rick's hospitality the way I have. Besides, I have to be back at work on the ninth or lose my job."

"It's just a job," Elizabeth pointed out. "A smart girl like you can always find another. And if it's money you're worried about, don't. You can come live with me until you find something."

"I can't do that, either. I didn't come here because I wanted money from you."

"I know that. But at least consider my offer. I'd love for you to stay with me for a while."

JENNY DID CONSIDER her offer, considered it very seriously, but in the end decided it was better that she not force herself on these generous people and decided to go back to West Texas where she really belonged. She had come to East Texas with only one goal in mind and she had met that goal. It was now time for her to leave.

Saturday night, while she busied herself packing her things, a deep sense of melancholy washed over her. Although she was certain she was doing the right thing by leaving, she was not entirely happy with her decision to go. She could barely swallow around the ache that filled her throat.

When Rick appeared in her room shortly after nine, she had gone from feeling sadly forlorn to feeling downright miserable. Although she had promised to visit often and fully intended to fulfill that promise, she was aware of how dreadfully she would miss these people during the times in between.

"Still determined to leave, I see," Rick said, looking just as miserable as she felt.

"Can't stay here living off you forever," she said, trying to keep her tone light. She did not want him to know that her heart was breaking.

"Why not?" he asked, stepping closer. "Why can't you stay here and live off me forever? It's not **like** I can't afford it."

"Because it would not be right. And because people would talk."

"Why does that bother you so? First you were worried what people would say about us when they discovered the common link we have in Mother, and now you worry what they might say if you continued to live here indefinitely. If people are going to consider us brother and sister, like you seem to think, then they aren't going to think much about us living in the same house. Besides, Mother said you could live in her house for a while, if it really bothers you that much."

"I can't do that. I don't expect you to understand why."

Rick's dour expression became even more glum. "Then I don't get to see you again until Thanksgiving?"

"I guess not."

"But that may be too late," he said suddenly coming up with what he felt was a clever idea.

"Too late for what?" She glanced at him, clearly puzzled. Suddenly she worried that there was something about Elizabeth's health that they had not told her.

"Jenny, you have to stay here and marry me," he said, ignoring her question as he reached for her shoulders and turned her to face him directly.

When Jenny noticed the serious expression on his face when he mentioned marriage, she blinked with further confusion, her heart filling with sudden hope. Although she wasn't too sure it would work out for the best, she found the thought of marrying Rick was downright thrilling. "What did you say?"

"I said that you *have* to stay here and marry me," he repeated, looking as serious as ever. "After all, it is the only decent thing for you to do."

"And why do you say that?" she wanted to know, as shocked as she was confused by such a sudden and peculiar proposal of marriage. Although they had discussed her staying, and had discussed the fact that they cared deeply for one another, marriage had never been deliberated. "Why would marrying you be the decent thing to do?"

Rick hung his head, as if terribly ashamed of what he had to say next, then announced in a soft but very serious-sounding voice, "I think I might be pregnant and I really don't want to put the child up for adoption."

Aware he was both teasing and at the same time serious, she decided to play along, curious to find out where such a strange conversation might lead. "And why wouldn't you want to put the child up for adoption? We were both adopted and look how great our lives turned out. We couldn't be happier."

"Oh, yes, we could," he insisted. His tone became truly serious when he stepped forward and gently took her into his arms, sending a shock wave of excitement through her. "That is, if you would just agree to marry me."

"But we hardly know each other," she pointed out, though she was already considering it as a very real and very thrilling possibility. "We only met a month and a half ago."

"Mother and Dad only knew each other two months before they were married," he pointed out. "And they ended up with one really terrific marriage."

"Ah, but they had two whole months to get to know each other." By now she was smiling, aware she liked the idea more and more. Although barely a year ago she'd sworn never to marry again, she knew it would be so different with Rick. Because he was different. He was like no one else.

"Okay," Rick finally conceded, looking deep into her glimmering brown eyes. "If you really want to be stubborn about it, take another two weeks. It will undoubtedly be sheer torture for me, but I can probably survive fourteen more days before marrying you."

"I don't know that you've really thought this thing through too well," she said, then bit her lower lip to contain her excitement. If Rick was really serious, and he had indeed thought it through, she just might be willing to say yes. She certainly loved him enough to want to spend the rest of her life with him, and she loved Rachel, too.

"I'll have you know I have given this considerable thought," he protested, eager for her to know the truth. "In fact, for the past week, I've thought of little else."

"But we'd be facing a lot of problems, problems I'm sure you have not yet considered," she continued, her eyes wide with the many thoughts racing through her mind.

"Like what?"

"Like the wedding itself. Don't you realize how much trouble we'd have with the seating arrangements?"

Rick knitted his brow, truly perplexed. "What sort of problems could we possibly have with seating?"

"Our mother," she reminded him with a playful grin. "Should she be seated as the mother of the bride or the mother of the groom? She can't possibly be on both sides at the same time."

Rick chuckled, not having considered that at all. "The way she likes always being in the middle of everything, we'll just let her stand in the very center of the aisle, right behind us. She'd love that." He laughed louder, while he considered the situation further. "Just think, if you agree to marry me, your own mother would end up also being your mother-in-law. Not many people would be able to say that."

"You would," she pointed out. "Because she would become *your* mother-in-law, too."

Rick's eyes twinkled when he pulled her firmly against him, certain she was about to say yes to marrying him. "Mind-boggling, isn't it?" He dipped down to steal a sweet kiss from her smiling lips. "It will take us a lifetime to sort it all out so it makes sense."

"A lifetime, indeed," she commented, then pulled his mouth back down to hers for a far more demanding kiss, one that would forever seal the promise of marriage she was about to make.

HARLEQUIN
American Romance®

COMING NEXT MONTH

#413 CHASING TROUBLE by Anne Stuart

San Francisco heiress Sally MacArthur knew she needed to hire a hard-boiled detective to find her half sister Lucy, who had run off with a mobster. Sally expected an adventure when she joined private investigator James Diamond but she didn't expect to find a diamond in the rough.

#414 RACING WITH THE MOON by Muriel Jensen

Genny Scott had a secret she'd guarded her entire life. Even her young daughter didn't know what she lived with from day to day. When Jack Fleming, a man determined to capture her heart, found out the truth, he surprised Genny with an interesting proposition. And for once in her life she didn't know what to do....

#415 RUNNING ON EMPTY by Kay Wilding

Elizabeth Bartlett, the bank president's daughter, and Cal Potts, the bad boy from the wrong side of the tracks, had shared a forbidden love as teens. Ten years later, Elizabeth discovered that coming back home is never easy, especially when old flames still burn.

#416 HOME IN HIS ARMS by Suzanne Simmons Guntrum

Jessie Jordan couldn't shake the feeling that she'd met Mitch Jade before. But the gentle Quaker and the fiery reporter were strangers... until destiny brought them together in a single, explosive moment that would change them forever.

HARLEQUIN®
OFFICIAL SWEEPSTAKES RULES

NO PURCHASE NECESSARY

1. To enter, complete an Official Entry Form or 3"× 5" index card by hand-printing, in plain block letters, your complete name, address, phone number and age, and mailing it to: Harlequin Fashion A Whole New You Sweepstakes, P.O. Box 9056, Buffalo, NY 14269-9056.

   No responsibility is assumed for lost, late or misdirected mail. Entries must be sent separately with first class postage affixed, and be received no later than December 31, 1991 for eligibility.

2. Winners will be selected by D.L. Blair, Inc., an independent judging organization whose decisions are final, in random drawings to be held on January 30, 1992 in Blair, NE at 10:00 a.m. from among all eligible entries received.

3. The prizes to be awarded and their approximate retail values are as follows: Grand Prize — A brand-new Mercury Sable LS plus a trip for two (2) to Paris, including round-trip air transportation, six (6) nights hotel accommodation, a $1,400 meal/spending money stipend and $2,000 cash toward a new fashion wardrobe (approximate value: $28,000) or $15,000 cash; two (2) Second Prizes — A trip to Paris, including round-trip air transportation, six (6) nights hotel accommodation, a $1,400 meal/spending money stipend and $2,000 cash toward a new fashion wardrobe (approximate value: $11,000) or $5,000 cash; three (3) Third Prizes — $2,000 cash toward a new fashion wardrobe. All prizes are valued in U.S. currency. Travel award air transportation is from the commercial airport nearest winner's home. Travel is subject to space and accommodation availability, and must be completed by June 30, 1993. Sweepstakes offer is open to residents of the U.S. and Canada who are 21 years of age or older as of December 31, 1991, except residents of Puerto Rico, employees and immediate family members of Torstar Corp., its affiliates, subsidiaries, and all agencies, entities and persons connected with the use, marketing, or conduct of this sweepstakes. All federal, state, provincial, municipal and local laws apply. Offer void wherever prohibited by law. Taxes and/or duties, applicable registration and licensing fees, are the sole responsibility of the winners. Any litigation within the province of Quebec respecting the conduct and awarding of a prize may be submitted to the Régie des loteries et courses du Québec. All prizes will be awarded; winners will be notified by mail. No substitution of prizes is permitted.

4. Potential winners must sign and return any required Affidavit of Eligibility/Release of Liability within 30 days of notification. In the event of noncompliance within this time period, the prize may be awarded to an alternate winner. Any prize or prize notification returned as undeliverable may result in the awarding of that prize to an alternate winner. By acceptance of their prize, winners consent to use of their names, photographs or their likenesses for purposes of advertising, trade and promotion on behalf of Torstar Corp. without further compensation. Canadian winners must correctly answer a time-limited arithmetical question in order to be awarded a prize.

5. For a list of winners (available after 3/31/92), send a separate stamped, self-addressed envelope to: Harlequin Fashion A Whole New You Sweepstakes, P.O. Box 4694, Blair, NE 68009.

PREMIUM OFFER TERMS

To receive your gift, complete the Offer Certificate according to directions. Be certain to enclose the required number of "Fashion A Whole New You" proofs of product purchase (which are found on the last page of every specially marked "Fashion A Whole New You" Harlequin or Silhouette romance novel). Requests must be received no later than December 31, 1991. Limit: four (4) gifts per name, family, group, organization or address. Items depicted are for illustrative purposes only and may not be exactly as shown. Please allow 6 to 8 weeks for receipt of order. Offer good while quantities of gifts last. In the event an ordered gift is no longer available, you will receive a free, previously unpublished Harlequin or Silhouette book for every proof of purchase you have submitted with your request, plus a refund of the postage and handling charge you have included. Offer good in the U.S. and Canada only.

HQFW-SWPR

HARLEQUIN® OFFICIAL
SWEEPSTAKES ENTRY FORM

4-FWARS-3

Complete and return this Entry Form immediately – the more entries you submit, the better your chances of winning!

- Entries must be received by **December 31, 1991.**
- A Random draw will take place on **January 30, 1992.**
- No purchase necessary.

Yes, I want to win a FASHION A WHOLE NEW YOU Classic and Romantic prize from Harlequin:

Name _____ Telephone _____ Age _____

Address _____

City _____ State _____ Zip _____

Return Entries to: **Harlequin FASHION A WHOLE NEW YOU,**
P.O. Box 9056, Buffalo, NY 14269-9056   © 1991 Harlequin Enterprises Limited

PREMIUM OFFER

To receive your free gift, send us the required number of proofs-of-purchase from any specially marked FASHION A WHOLE NEW YOU Harlequin or Silhouette Book with the Offer Certificate properly completed, plus a check or money order (do not send cash) to cover postage and handling payable to Harlequin FASHION A WHOLE NEW YOU Offer. We will send you the specified gift.

OFFER CERTIFICATE

Item	A. ROMANTIC COLLECTOR'S DOLL	B. CLASSIC PICTURE FRAME
	(Suggested Retail Price $60.00)	(Suggested Retail Price $25.00)
# of proofs-of-purchase	18	12
Postage and Handling	$3.50	$2.95
Check one	☐	☐

Name _____

Address _____

City _____ State _____ Zip _____

Mail this certificate, designated number of proofs-of-purchase and check or money order for postage and handling to: **Harlequin FASHION A WHOLE NEW YOU Gift Offer,** P.O. Box 9057, Buffalo, NY 14269-9057. Requests must be received by December 31, 1991.

ONE
PROOF-OF-PURCHASE

4-FWARP-3

To collect your fabulous free gift you must include the necessary number of proofs-of-purchase with a properly completed Offer Certificate.

© 1991 Harlequin Enterprises Limited

See previous page for details.